For Joanna

VOLCANIC JESUS

HAWAIIAN TALES

LEE A. JACOBUS

HAMMONASSET HOUSE

Hammonasset House Books, LLC

Mystic, Connecticut 06355
http://hammonassethouse.com

Library of Congress Control Number 2007909929
Library of Congress Cataloging in Publication Data

I. Jacobus, Lee A., 1935-
II. Title

ISBN-13: 978-0-9801894-4-5
Manufactured in the United States

1. Fiction–short stories   2. Fiction–Literary
3. Fiction–General
I. Title

VOLCANIC JESUS

HAWAIIAN TALES

Pi'ilani, the Girl with Heavenly Eyes 7

An Angel of Supermanagement 25

A View of the Ocean 45

Having Lost 66

Volcanic Jesus 80

Never Turn Your Back on the Sea 113

The Menehune 130

Why Not Live at the Hokele? 144

Is God Calling You? 166

Old Bones 188

Pi'ilani, The Girl With Heavenly Eyes

P i'ilani lived with Kela in Auntie Peg's old house, a low-slung bungalow with a patched tin roof that Auntie Peg used to call the Koloa sieve, although it leaked only when the wind was northerly. The stucco walls radiated a red-dirt glow in the sunset and showed its cracks in the early morning sun, when Pi'ilani sometimes stood in the open doorway hoping the new day was truly a new day.

Pi'ilani was Auntie Peg's favorite grandchild. It was no secret. Auntie Peg would coo to her, "You my sweetie little hula girl," when Pi'ilani danced the hula in her third grade school festivals. She sang for Auntie Peg while Auntie Peg was bedridden in the room where she and Kela now slept. "Going to the Hokey Luau, Hokey Hokey Luau." She swayed rhythmically and moved her hands in the sea-waving motion she loved as she danced and saw the smile spread over Auntie Peg's toothless face. She was very sweet, Auntie Peg, and without her teeth she seemed like a wrinkled baby gasping for air, laughing and sighing. Auntie Peg had always lived in the house on Piku Street in Po'ipu, where the haole came and made the mansions and the resorts that closed the town from the sea. No one ever offered to buy her house the way they had bought the Tanakas' great shack on the high ground near the public beach. The Tanakas left Po'ipu for one of the condos in Princeville. And they left rich. Auntie Peg's house stood forlorn and shabby, with the sagging screen door and the rusting window frames–just as it had been when Auntie Peg died and Pi'ilani discovered that it was hers. All she had to do was move in.

At first Pi'ilani thought people had made a mistake, or worse that they were making fun of her. She was a small, slender woman with cocoa skin, long black hair, and full, romantic lips. When Auntie Peg died she was only eighteen and still dreamed of strong, long-haired men swimming toward her in a fantasy of love that she knew, truly, would never be hers. She stood there without saying a word when she was told about the house. After she saw how angry her sister Ku'ana grew when she heard what Auntie Peg had done–and had done legally with Stuart Hepplewhite, the lawyer in Waimea–Pi'ilani began to take things seriously.

Ku'ana was ten years older, darker and more threatening. She was already married and had two children, Betty-ma and Linda-ma, and lived in the same house with her husband Kana's parents. Kana Medeiros supervised the burn-away in the sugar fields that provided some of the island's electricity. He was a very important man, but he didn't think he could afford his own place. Ku'ana hated Kana's parents even though they had given her and Kana the biggest room in the house and stayed home with Betty-ma and Linda-ma while Ku'ana worked in the restaurants in Po'ipu, where people told her she was so lovely and so polite.

Pi'ilani almost cried when Ku'ana told her she did not deserve her own house, even such a shacky wreck as Auntie Peg's. "It's not so shacky," Pi'ilani said.

"Worse," Ku'ana told her. "In a big wind you'll be left sitting on the wicker couch and end up getting a sunburn. You'll see."

Mama Opa settled things for Pi'ilani with a single sentence. "Auntie Peg said so." That was all she needed to tell Ku'ana. And instead of turning the house over to Ku'ana and her family, Pi'ilani moved her few things out of Mama Opa's and down the street to Auntie Peg's. Mama Opa cried as if Pi'ilani were leaving the island, the way Mama cried when her sons Duke and Ho'okipa decided to go to college in Oahu and left the island essentially forever. Duke was an eye doctor in San Diego and Ho'okipa settled on the big island running a business for a mainland consortium whose complications he could never explain. They sometimes called to talk with Mama Opa, but Pi'ilani never knew what they talked about. She read their postcards and their Christmas cards, but she knew little of their lives.

Kana and Ku'ana didn't talk to Pi'ilani for more than a month. But after that, Ku'ana waged a fierce war with Kana until he finally gave up and moved them out of his parents' house and into a second floor apartment on the main street of Hanapepe. Ku'ana told everyone she was taking art lessons and that one of the galleries said she had enough talent to be an important native painter.

Pi'ilani knew what a native painter was, but she wondered if Ku'ana knew–given the way she told people. Ku'ana was good with a paint brush and in a way really gifted with her children. She and the children often made water color paintings together in the evenings when Ku'ana took time off from work. Now that she and Kana were paying rent, though, there was less time, and Ku'ana needed to drop the children off at Kana's parents' place after school when she worked the dinner shift. The Medeiroses kept the children's old room much as it was, so the children sometimes slept overnight. Mama Medeiros affected annoyance at this arrangement, but everyone knew she loved her grandchildren much more than she had ever loved her own. If Ku'ana was going to be a native painter and show her work in Hanapepe, she was going to have a hard time of it.

Or at least that's what Pi'ilani thought. While she got herself settled in Auntie Peg's house she looked around for a job. She could now work almost anywhere on the island because with the house she also got Auntie Peg's ancient skyblue Ford Falcon. Ho'okipa taught her to drive when she was fourteen and now with her license she was free as a dove. She thought first that she would get a job at the Hyatt, where she had cleaned rooms after school. But the Hyatt was not taking people on. The woman in the office talked with Pi'ilani and seemed alarmed when she asked for a job cleaning rooms. "My goodness," the woman said. "My goodness, no. You have heavenly eyes. You should think of something else." But what else? Someone said she should try the Academy of Tourism. That's where the jobs were. But she did not have any money except for the tiny sum Auntie Peg had left her. It would not last long. In the time it took Pi'ilani to find a decent job working for Budget Rental cars, Ku'ana had produced enough paintings to have a show at one of the smallest of the galleries on the main street of Hanapepe. It was not quite a miracle, but it was close. That's what Mama Opa said. Mama Medeiros said nothing. But when Kana told her how much money the tourists paid for her work her expression changed and everyone knew that Mama Medeiros thought the tourists were even crazier than they used to be when she was a girl and watched the cars stop on Po'ipu Road and the women get out with clippers and snip off the red hibiscus from the Kamanas' hedge–which always had the worst flowers in the neighborhood.

On Pi'ilani's first day of work they told her to park her car far away, out of sight because it might discourage the customers. Mr. Edwards also told her where to go to get the car washed after work, something she had meant to do earlier, but her ipa, Kela, decided to move in with her in Auntie Peg's house and needed $3.50 for a guitar string , so she gave him the money she might have used to make the Ford look presentable. Mr. Edwards also told her that she should get a dress like Tori Ishagawa's, something bright and cheerful with flowers on it. The tourists liked that. She said she would get one when she could. She did not tell him that she had only one dress and that her only option was to raid Auntie Peg's closet for one of her old dress-up church gowns.

Except for Mr. Edwards she would never have thought to look in the closet because Auntie Peg mainly had a collection of dowdy mu-mu's. But deep in the closet she found some bright dresses that seemed almost unworn. When Auntie Peg died she was a big woman, almost fat, but you never called her fat. When she was in a good mood she called herself "substantial," which seemed to mean the same thing. But these dresses were not for a fat Auntie Peg. They were bright yellows, greens, reds, blues, like the lobelia and lehua. When Pi'ilani took the dresses out, she hung them in the sun and brushed them down. They were surprising and cheerful, not like what Auntie Peg usually wore. Pi'ilani had never seen her in these dresses. Auntie Peg could never fit into them. But they fit Pi'ilani perfectly.

When she appeared the next day at the Budget counter Mr. Edwards nodded to her and said he approved. Tori Ishagawa loved the yellow dress she decided to wear first. It was China silk with a wavy hem and sleeves with large orange and red ilima flowers repeated from front to back. Tori picked up the hem and held it out to see the whole pattern. "Ooh," she said, "a vintage dress. You get it at Castaways?" Pi'ilani didn't say it was Auntie Peg's dress or that she found it in the back of the closet and had hung it out in the evening air. All she said was, "No, it's mine."

"Must have been your mama's," Tori told her. "You don't see those no more except in Castaways. Very expensive. You didn't get it there?" Pi'ilani shook her head and Mr. Edwards came to give her more training so she could do her job, finding vouchers, upgrades, where the keys should go (in the trunk keyhole) and how to work the machines for the credit cards. She was able to do it all by the second day and she felt happy knowing that in two weeks she would have more money and could help Kela buy the new guitar he wanted.

When Kela came back from having his Chevy pickup looked at in Anahola it was dark and Pi'ilani had put on her old dress and had her dinner and decided to lie down. Her feet hurt her from standing all day, but she knew she would get used to it in time. "Any dinner for me?" Kela said. He put his guitar in the corner and went to the fridge. He saw a piece of cooked Ono and some rice on a plate.

Pi'ilani came to the kitchen. "You had a good time?"

"Benny's crazy sonabitch. But, yeah. We played outside his

garage. Some people stopped by in their cars. Said it was good. He says he's gonna use me maybe when he plays in Hanalei. Sonny Kahu is maybe gonna work on the big island starting this week. That's what Benny says. So he's gonna take me on he says."

"That's nice. How's the truck?"

"We gotta put a shock on it. Cost us eighty dollars T'ko says. He'll do it when you get paid. What do I do with this?" He pointed to the fish and rice. Pi'ilani took the dish and warmed it in the oven. Kela smelled of beer and she knew not to tell him she didn't like the smell. She looked at the tattoos on his arm, some almost starting to fade. Some were Chinese, with meanings that Kela had forgotten. And on the back of his neck was his name in capital letters. She liked his tattoos and once had a small red lehua tattooed below her collarbone. Mama Opa scowled but never scolded her. It was Pi'ilani's money, after all.

"You tired?" she asked.

"Hungry, woman, hungry. Benny says we gonna play a gig. Pay me some money, too." He went to the fridge and took out a bottle of beer. He made a gesture toward her, but she held up her hand. "Work tomorrow," she said.

"Always work," he said, not looking at her.

They heard the light tapping of rain on the roof and Pi'ilani looked out the window at the palm tree by the driveway. There was no wind, just the light patter of large rain drops in the night. When Kela settled into his chair and began eating his dinner, she moved back to the bedroom and fell asleep.

Kela went to Lihue to buy his guitar. Pi'ilani gave him $540, virtually all she had earned. He took his old guitar with him and traded it in, although he said he only got $40 for it. "Piece of junk," he told her, holding it in one hand as if he were about to shatter it. When he rattled back in the Chevy pickup he plugged in his new amplifier and played her part of a Beach Boys song.

"Is that what Benny Wong likes?" she asked.

"They like that in Hanalei. And the blues." He began vamping loudly and started singing, "When you got the low-down blues . . . ."

She had heard this kind of music before when Kela sat, cigarette dangling from his lips, eyes half-closed in concentration, mumbling words and striking loud chords. But it never meant very much to her. Sometimes when he signaled for another beer she would bring him a Budweiser from Auntie Peg's Fridgidaire and he would sing more blues. Other times, Pi'ilani would go outside where the air was clear and the sky radiant. She could still hear Kela intoning his song. But things outside were calmer and he had to get his own Budweiser.

Pi'ilani's heart sank when he told her that he had only paid for part of the cost of his guitar. "It's a Fender, man," he said. And he said they had until next month to get the other $600. Pi'ilani wondered how this instrument, which was clearly used and not new, could cost three weeks of her work with Budget Rent-a-Car.

"Hey," Kela said. "Hey, I gonna make a few dollars in Hanalei. You'll see. With Benny's band. Man, he's gonna pay me after every gig."

Tori Ishagawa was normally supercritical. What Pi'ilani didn't like was the way she weaseled news out of her. When she explained how important Kela's guitar was to him Tori just laughed. "You got a problem," she told her. Pi'ilani wished a customer would show up and force Tori to get back to work. Mr. Edwards came in and gave Pi'ilani some papers and keys and told her to drive the Econoline over to the Aston in Po'ipu. She was grateful and smiled for the first time that day. She listened to the radio and found a station playing Kei'li Reichel singing the kind of music she liked, soft

13

Hawaiian-sounding tunes full of sentiment and hopefulness.

But when she got back Tori caught up with her and quizzed her about Kela. "He don't work?" she asked.

"He's a musician."

"Lives off you, huh? That right?"

Pi'ilani didn't want to answer. Kela never had a job that she knew of. He smoked cigarettes, drank beer, and played the guitar. Sometimes he was nice to her, but usually that was before they went to bed. Then he'd go to sleep and snore so loud she would go into the kitchen for the night. But those nights were rare these days. Usually he was out. Now that the band was playing at Hanalei she saw even less of him than she used to. He came home when she was asleep and she heard him sometimes play his guitar without the amplifier. She knew he was drunk by the way he shuffled across the kitchen floor, but she never said anything.

"Then they always drinkin'," Tori told her after a customer left with the keys to one of the Mustang 5-liter convertibles. "Like that haole there." The man did not look as if he had been drinking, although his face was very red and he was so large that she wondered how he would fit into the car. "I bet your Kela drinks too much."

Pi'ilani wished Tori Ishigawa would keep quiet about Kela. She wished she had never said a word to her about him, but everything came out one morning when Pi'ilani showed up at work with a black eye. Mr. Edwards didn't notice because lately he never looked directly at Tori or Pi'ilani. He just gave his papers, keys, and orders to one of them and turned away. Tori said he was worried about his job. Tori seemed to know everything.

"Girl, you gotta do something about that man," Tori told her emphatically. She stood with hands on her hips and glared at her. Pi'ilani didn't want to look her in the eye, so she stared at the orchid behind her ear. Mr. Edwards asked them both to wear orchids behind their ear.

Pi'ilani cried. She didn't want to, but the tears came anyway. Her right eye hurt where Kela hit her. She explained that he was drunk and didn't mean it. Things had gone bad for him and he was playing with his new guitar which broke a string, and he just got mad and turned too fast and his elbow . . . .

Tori screwed up her face. "That's no attitude. Get rid of him. No man ever hit me twice."

"He won't hit me again. It was an accident."

Tori laughed cynically before she could say another word. "I heard that before," she said.

"Really."

Tori laughed again and Pi'ilani was grateful to say "Aloha," to a man who came to the counter fumbling for his voucher. She let Tori take him and she went behind the counter pretending to be doing something important.

Later that night Ku'ana came by with Betty-ma and Linda-ma and Pi'ilani tried to keep in the shadows when they came in the house.

"Hey, who gave you the black eye?" Ku'ana asked. "You walk into a door?"

"Yes," Pi'ilani said.

"That's bull," Ku'ana said, pulling her over to the light. Pi'ilani noticed that Ku'ana was beginning to become substantial like Auntie Peg. "What did that man do to you? Look at that, will you? Let me tell you Kana never done that to me. Never. Never let him, neither. What's the matter with you, girl? This place needs fixin'. Don't he fix nothin' around here? What's he doin'? Kana saw him in Hanalei just sittin' around on the bench near Tropical Turmoil. What's he doin'?"

Pi'ilani explained how he was out there so he could play in the band with Benny Wong. Her voice was soft, so soft Ku'ana asked her again. "Speak up," she said as if she were Mama Opa.

When Kela went to Lihue to pay off his new guitar, Pi'ilani's eye was almost back to normal and she thought that their life would be happy and that Kela would fix up the house and fix the Chevy and fix their life together. But when she got home from work Kela was not there and the house seemed sad and empty. Pi'ilani looked at the table in front of the old wicker settee in the front room and decided to straighten the papers and throw out the old bottles. Auntie Peg had always tried to make the house look decent. Pi'ilani remembered how Auntie Peg sat in the soft green chair she loved next to her parrot's beak plant. She would laugh and tell Pi'ilani she was like an angel in her life, how her smile made Auntie Peg feel good all over. Auntie Peg was always grateful when Pi'ilani made her a nice dinner with lomilomi and rice and strong coffee. "You gonna get an ipa of your own, you'll see," Auntie Peg told her when she was little. Pi'ilani had wondered whether Auntie Peg had her own ipa, and when she asked, Auntie Peg laughed very loud and very long. "I had my ipa long ago, girl, long ago."

Pi'ilani went through Auntie Peg's personal box and found some sepia photographs that surprised her. One of them showed a young man standing on the running board of an old convertible. He had a big grin on his face and flexed his arms like a prize fighter. His hair was spiky and dark and his shirt hung from the rear view mirror. In another photo a young woman with beautiful eyes and perfect teeth smiled back at her and it was only after a moment that Pi'ilani realized it was Auntie Peg when she was a girl. She was wearing the dress Tori Ishigawa thought was so wonderful. And in yet another of the photographs the same young man with a cowrie necklace and beautiful shoulders sat next to her in an open car. The man smiled at the camera and pulled Auntie Peg toward him in an attempt at an embrace. He was Auntie Peg's ipa. But what had happened to him? There were no more photographs of him, and nothing else in the box that gave a hint about him except for one tarnished brass button that had small crossed rifles on it. A button that had come from an army uniform, Pi'ilani thought. It must have been his. Auntie Peg never talked about him and never mentioned his name.

At the bottom of the box she found a small brown calendar book that seemed to be from a hotel. Pi'ilani opened it and saw an entry for the date, October 15, 1948. All the pages before that date had been torn out. On that page Auntie Peg had written: "Robt bring his car yello dress." Pi'ilani turned the page, and saw another entry: "Robt tonite." Each page had space for seven entries, one for each day of the week. Pi'ilani turned each page and saw that each Friday there was a small entry: "Robt Red Dres," "Robt blue Dres," until she got to the last page, where she saw "Robt green drs" with a line through it. It was a wavy line that seemed to eradicate the whole entry. What had happened?

The writing on the last page was difficult to read. Auntie Peg had used a pencil which left a smudgy, light stroke that ultimately trailed off where a corner had been torn away. As far as she could make it out, Auntie Peg had written, "Robt. hert my felings. I wated and wated. Took and broke my car. Took and broke my hart. Took . . .," but after that nothing was legible.

She closed the book and looked at it. The cover once had a raised imprint of a hotel, although the gilding had worn away so that she could not quite make it out. Somehow, Pi'ilani hoped there would be more. "Robt" must have been short for Robert. The man in the photograph? He must have been her ipa. Pi'ilani smiled to herself with the thought that her Auntie Peg could have had a sweetheart in 1948 and that she could have worn her yellow dress in the convertible car in the photograph. But she worried, too, knowing that it must have been her ipa who hurt her, who broke her heart. What had he done to hurt her so? And what had she done to put him out of her life? Pi'ilani searched through the box and found a book for 1949, but there was no mention of "Robt." Every so often in January and

February Auntie Peg had noted something interesting, like "Goin to Opa's" or "Suppr tonite." But the entries ended in the middle of February and there were no more marks of any kind after that. Pi'ilani closed the box and pushed it back in the closet. She kept out the photographs and studied them again. Something about the young man's smile she didn't like.

A few nights later Ku'ana parked on the side of the house and came in with one of her paintings. "For your living room," she said, and Pi'ilani realized she was not sarcastic. She was giving her a present. The painting was not very large, but it was nice. The flowers were yellow and the background was a rich green, broad leaves and dark stems. Everything was a bit fatter than it might have been in reality, but the effect was pleasant. Ku'ana helped Pi'ilani find the hammer and a nail and they hung it over the settee where the late morning sunlight always brightened the room.

Pi'ilani thanked her and told her how nice the painting was.

"Where's he at tonight?" Ku'ana asked, looking around for Kela.

"He plays with the band in Hanalei."

"I bet. Who painted the kitchen?" Pi'ilani didn't answer. "You did it, huh? How'd you get the time? Rent-a-Car business gettin' slow?"

"I had time."

"It's brighter. I like it."

Pi'ilani made her sister some coffee. "You ever hear anything about Auntie Peg's boyfriend?" she asked.

Ku'ana laughed. "Boyfriend? Auntie Peg never had no boyfriend."

Pi'ilani showed her the photographs and the calendar book. Ku'ana stared at the photo of the young man, and then the book. She shook her head slowly while she studied the photo of the young man

18

and woman in the convertible. "You sure this is Auntie Peg?"

"Look," she said, and pointed to the large rings on the woman's right hand. They were on Auntie Peg's hand when she was buried. They both looked at the photograph and Ku'ana whistled softly through her teeth.

"I never heard about this," Ku'ana said. "No one never said nothing about this. All the years she worked sewing for Mrs. Harare I never heard and Mama never said."

"Would Mama have known?"

Ku'ana shook her head. "Maybe not. Hey, maybe nobody knew. You got any more photos of that guy?"

Pi'ilani brought out another box that Auntie Peg kept in the closet in her bedroom. It was sealed with paper tape that almost crumbled under her fingers. They both went through the old papers and clippings and some old dress patterns Auntie Peg had saved without ever opening. But there were no photographs, no books, no measure of a personal life in anything in the box. And there were no more boxes.

"Throw that stuff out," Ku'ana said. "It's garbage. That photo's probably from a blind date or something. That's what she meant by her waiting and waiting. I don't know. But I don't think anybody ever was Auntie Peg's sweetheart."

Pi'ilani didn't say anything. It was always useless to argue with Ku'ana. So instead, she listened to Ku'ana tell her how people were buying her paintings and how she made Kana spend the weekend fixing the plumbing in the apartment so they could take a shower when they wanted. When she and Kana took the apartment Pi'ilani helped them move and was surprised to find the second floor over the restaurant was bigger than Auntie Peg's house and much brighter. The windows were old fashioned and went down almost to the floor. Ku'ana explained how the gallery told her she needed the right light to paint. She had no idea if it was the right light, but it was a lot of light.

Most of Ku'ana's paintings were strange to Pi'ilani. They were usually of children, large, robust, and round children with oversize hands holding plaintive dolls. The children had large eyes with dark pupils that followed you when you walked from side to side in front of the painting. They had toys on the floor in front of them, but they didn't seem to notice them. Something about their look told Pi'ilani that they were not really there in the painting–they just appeared to be there. The children seemed to have no soul, no matter how much their eyes followed you across the room.

"I think this was Auntie Peg's ipa," Pi'ilani finally said. "I think he hurt her very much." They both looked at the photo.

"Yeah, maybe," Ku'ana agreed. "What about your ipa? Where's he at?"

"Hanalei, I told you."

"Let's go see."

Pi'ilani didn't want to go anywhere. She was tired and told Ku'ana she didn't see any point in it, but Ku'ana took her by the arm and put her in the pickup Kana got her and they began up the highway to the north shore. They went through the tunnel of trees without a word and all Pi'ilani could think was that Ku'ana would be surprised when she heard how well Kela learned to play the tunes the tourists liked to hear.

The sky had darkened by the time they got to Princeville and the lights out toward the ocean glowed rich and golden. In Hanalei a few people were standing on the veranda in front of Bubba's outdoor stand waiting for their hamburgers. Ku'ana steered the car into the Big Save parking lot and pulled up with a fierce attack on the brakes. "I don't hear no music," she said.

It was true. They heard the sound of cars, of people in the restaurants nearby, but no music. They got out and crossed the road and went behind Bubba's to the Gourmet Restaurant and looked in the

20

open door. People were talking and shouting and drinking and against the wall they saw a set of drums, a microphone, and several guitars on their stands. One of them was Kela's Fender, just standing there with nobody near it. Pi'ilani stared at it. "They're takin' a break," Ku'ana said. "Must be."

Pi'ilani looked around for Benny Wong, but neither he nor T'ko or Kela were in the room. They saw a waiter come with a tray full of food and set things down on a nearby table. Ku'ana went to him and asked where the band was.

"Back in ten, he says. Let's take a look." Ku'ana took her by the arm and steered her out to the walkway and toward the nearby fancy restaurant and shopping area that they built to look like a Tahitian villa. But they took only a few steps, when Ku'ana suddenly turned around and headed in the other direction toward the public parking area on the far side of Bubba's. It was protected by a stand of trees and lighted by a small dim lamppost. As they approached, they both heard some laughing and a bottle break on the macadam. Pi'ilani saw Kela's Chevy pickup, and was glad in her heart when she saw it empty. But Ku'ana pointed to an old Volvo station wagon parked in the darkest section of the lot. They heard Kela's laughter come from the car, then a curse and more laughter. They came very close to the car, but no one inside noticed them. They saw Kela and T'ko, and two girls with their shirts off. It was not easy to see in the dark, but it was plain that they were half naked and laughing as if they were laughing at Ku'ana and Pi'ilani.

But no one in the car saw either of them. Pi'ilani shook loose from Ku'ana and ran back across the street stumbling and crying. At first Ku'ana stood near the Volvo and was going to shout at Kela, but after a moment she turned and ran after Pi'ilani. The two sisters stood by the car and neither spoke. Pi'ilani felt suddenly very much like a little girl whose big sister had just warned her not to go into the water and not to take chances. Ku'ana put her arm around Pi'ilani's

21

shoulder and held her for a long time.

On the drive home Ku'ana just told her to make up her mind. She had to do something, but she wasn't going to tell her what to do. "Mama Opa could tell you what to do, but I'm not going to do that." She drove a few miles on the twisty road. "But I know what I'd do."

Pi'ilani knew what to do, too. She wasn't sure she could do it, but she knew what she ought to do.

Back at Auntie Peg's house, Pi'ilani held the photograph of Auntie Peg and her ipa. Was there only one ipa for everyone, the way Pi'ilani always believed? Was Kela the only ipa she'd ever have? It was pretty clear he must have thought so. Pi'ilani used to fear that no one would want her as his ipa, but sometimes she saw boys looking at her in a way that made her wonder. Kela used to look at her that way, too. Pi'ilani touched her hand to her eye and felt it still tender. She put the photograph back in its box.

If Kela had come home that night he would have found his clothes piled out near the driveway. His box of tapes and CDs stood next to the clothes and a plastic suitcase with the rest of his things leaned to one side. Pi'ilani had made up her mind. When she reported for work Tori Ishigawa stared at her for a moment and asked was something wrong.

"No. Nothing wrong."

"That boy hit you again?" She took Pi'ilani by the shoulder and turned her toward her.

"Nobody's going to hit me," Pi'ilani said.

"So you kicked him out," Tori said with a slight note of triumph.

Pi'ilani took a stack of contracts from under the counter and riffled through them. She had four returned cars to process and she tried to look busy.

"Isn't that it? I bet you that's it." Tori took a set of keys from the out-board and jingled them while she watched Pi'ilani. "You much better off."

Later that afternoon Kela drove in with his Chevy. Pi'ilani looked at him as he climbed out of the truck. His things were scattered in the bed of the pickup. His shirt hung from the rear window and the muscles rippled under his brown skin. When he came up to her, she looked at him with lifeless eyes. "What'ch you doin', bitch? You coulda ruined my sheet music. If it rained it woulda ruined my fake book." He reached a hand out to grab her and she pulled back out of his grasp.

Mr. Edwards came out of the office and stood near her. "You okay?" he asked.

"Fine," Pi'ilani said.

"You looking for a rental car?" he asked Kela, as if he were an innocent bystander. Tori Ishigawa had followed Mr. Edwards out of the office and stared at Kela. As they stood there Kela seemed struck dumb.

"No," he finally said. "No."

A customer hit the service bell in the office. No one looked around. "Then?" Mr. Edwards said as if he were genuinely curious.

"I don't want no damned car," Kela said.

Mr. Edwards touched Pi'ilani gently on the forearm. "Would you get that customer?" The bell had rung again.

"Bye," Pi'ilani said to Kela as she turned to help the sweaty man who stood impatiently on the far side of the counter.

"Is that all you got to say?"

"We're working here," Mr. Edwards told him. "So if Pi'ilani says goodbye, that means it's time to go."

For an instant Kela came close to losing it. But something about the way Mr. Edwards put his last sentence and the way he bent his arm up to his chest made Kela turn around and leave. Later that night Kana sat in Auntie Peg's kitchen with Pi'ilani drinking Chinese

23

tea when Kela's truck pulled up on the lawn. Pi'ilani sat still while Kana went outside and talked to Kela. All she could hear was the wind rattling the soapberry bushes outside the window and against the dark blue sky she saw the Koa trees bending left and right as the wind picked up. There would be rain tonight.

Kana came back inside and Pi'ilani heard the Chevy rattle away. "He won't be back," Kana said. He went and poured another cup of tea. "You know, I like your house," Kana said when he sat down. "You're makin' it look real good. Betty-ma and Linda-ma tell me you a good cook. Not like your sister." He laughed and pulled out a cigarette. He held his lighter up to the wall where Pi'ilani tacked the sepia photograph of Auntie Peg. "This you?" He asked. When Pi'ilani told him who it was he looked at it again. "Sweet eyes," was all he said.

An Angel of Supermanagement

L ily Caceres had just finished making papier mache masks for the Menehune fete at Molokai School when she got the message to see Mr. Cisneros immediately. She gave the class to Madeline Kuriyama, the teaching intern from the university. Then she stepped into the teacher's bathroom and worked on the stiffened paste beneath her nails. She could do nothing with the sleeves of her blouse, so she left them alone rather than risk wetting them. She took just a moment to touch up her hair. Her mind was blank as she turned the corner into the office.

Mr. Cisneros stood with the phone in his hand. "Lily, it's your son Davos."

Lily brightened. Davos rarely ever called her at school. She reached out for it.

"No, I mean this is about Davos." He did not give her the phone.

"I . . . ." She could hardly speak.

"They have him down at the sub-station. He doesn't have any clothes."

Lilly looked at him and then averted her eyes. "My God, what?" But before she could say anything more, Mr. Cisneros went back to the phone saying he and Davos's mother would come right away. He asked the person on the other end not to do anything until he got there.

When they got to the sub-station on Kekui Street, Officer Palau told them he responded to a call saying Davos commanded the middle of the busy intersection on Beretainia Street, in front of the parking area for the supermarket. Davos directed traffic, but he had no clothes on except for a glistening white cape. Several drivers followed his gesturing arms into the parking lot without apparent surprise, but two women just out of the Times Supermarket refused to do what he told them and he smashed his hands flat on their hood. It was then they realized that not only did he have no shirt under his cape, but he also had no trousers. Among other things, they expressed concern, according to Officer Palau, that their ice cream would melt before they could get home. Davos would not let them move. He held one hand on their hood and signaled to the traffic with his other hand and imitated a police whistle with surprising accuracy.

Officer Palau could not get Davos away from the car by himself. Davos threatened him verbally, and Office Palau decided to wait for help. Davos was very big for eighteen and Officer Palau, with only six years to retirement, nursed an ailing hip. The doctor diagnosed it as trochanteric bursitis. On rainy days it acted up, and today was overcast. Officer Palau told Lily and Mr. Cisneros all this before letting her go to see her son. "He didn't get hurt," Officer Palau told her. "But I don't know what happened there. I tried to talk to him, but he didn't say anything that made any sense to me. We put him in one of the orange coveralls, so don't get the idea he's a criminal or anything. It's just that he needed some clothes. I've got Penny Medeiros watching him. He wouldn't calm down until I got a female officer to sit near him. We're worried, you know. Can't just leave him alone."

"Where are his clothes?" Lily asked.

"I didn't look for them. I was trying to keep him stable. That's the main thing with something like this. Keep him stable. He started to get a little mean out there, the way he was banging his hands on that Volvo. And with it looking like rain. I didn't dare take my eyes off him." Officer Palau moved behind his desk and lifted a plastic shopping bag from behind his chair and gave it to Mrs.

Caceres. She saw that it was Davos's white cape.

Davos left that morning with a beautiful blue shirt that Lily bought for him only last weekend. And his dark trousers, the ones he said he really liked so much–what happened to them? He probably wasn't wearing shoes, but surely he had his shirt and trousers with him. For an instant, Lily felt she ought to go and look for them.

"Is he stable now?" Mr. Cisneros asked.

"I don't know what to say, Dick. He was spouting a lot of weird stuff about being the Angel of Supermanagement or something. You ever hear of that?"

Lily gasped. She'd heard the words from Davos's lips and thought he was joking. "I need to see him," she said, pressing her small hands against Officer Palau's side as she tried to get by him.

"Okay, okay, but I have to warn you Mrs. Caceres. He's not himself. You gotta know that."

He was right. Davos was not himself. When Lily went down the corridor to where Penny Medeiros sat, she realized that they put Davos not in a room, but in a cell. And it was locked. "Davos," she said. She tried not to be panicky. She feared it might undo him. "Davos, are you all right?" Davos did not answer, and he did not look up. He rocked ceaselessly on his cot, his arms holding his knees tightly to his chest. His moaning began to fill the room. "Davos," she said urgently, the fear rising suddenly. She tried not to cry, but she could not contain herself. "Davos, what did you do?" But Davos only moaned like an injured soul.

"He's been doing this," Penny Medeiros said. "I tried to talk to him, but he won't speak."

Mr. Cisneros stayed behind with Officer Palau. Fortunately, he came each year to Molokai School to talk with students about drugs and law enforcement, so he recognized Davos and gave him special attention.

"We can't just let him go," Officer Palau told Lily as he led her back down the corridor. She had not been able to get Davos to respond with anything more than his soft moaning. She wanted to take him home immediately, but they would not even let her stay with Davos in his cell. "We've got a procedure where we have to call a doctor before we can do anything like let him go."

"Has he been hurt? I couldn't get a good look at him. He's all doubled over and won't look at me."

"Not that kind of doctor. We gotta get a psychiatrist in here before I can do anything with him. That's why Penny's sitting there. She's gotta watch him so's he doesn't hurt himself. It's the procedure, you see."

"He's not going to hurt himself." Lily tried not to sound indignant. "Why would he hurt himself? He does not need a psychologist." They obviously did not know Davos.

Both Officer Palau and Mr. Cisneros tried to comfort Lily, but she hardly heard them. She slumped into the wooden chair next to Officer Palau's desk. His computer hummed loudly and at her angle the screen flickered. She tried to think clearly, but her mind was a muddle. What had possessed Davos to go out on the street wearing only that cape? And what did he mean when he said he was the Angel of Supermanagement? She had told him the only angels were in the Bible. There were no angels in Honolulu. She was so happy when he found the summer job at the Times Supermarket in the fish department. He liked opening oysters and often brought home a few dimpled pearls which he saved in a tall caper bottle. They both enjoyed watching it slowly fill with iridescent jewels. Davos was such a good boy. Such a bright boy. He was a natural leader.

The state psychiatrist, Leonie Steinroe, a short, thickset woman of sixty or so presented herself in a sudden entrance from the hall. Her windblown hair was graying, her dark suit rumpled, and her old leather briefcase overflowed with yellow, blue, and white documents. She told Lily to stay put while she talked with Davos and insisted that Penny Medeiros let her into the cell so she could "reach" him, as she said. Lily protested that Davos did not need a psychiatrist. "My God," she said under her breath. "He doesn't need anything like that. He's just been under strain with getting ready for college. He needs some rest." She did not have a chance to tell Dr. Steinroe that Davos was president of the Chess Club, a member of the Science Pioneers, top of his class in math, and had an important part in the senior class play, "Mother Courage," which he memorized entirely near the end of rehearsals. She knew the problem. The boy was just tired. He needed to take a few days off and stop pushing himself so hard. Hadn't she suggested as much to Davos the time she found him sitting in his room in the dark staring at his empty chessboard?

Penny Medeiros came out and looked at Lily. "She's tough, but she's very good." She touched Lily's arm to comfort her. "Don't be scared of her."

Lily didn't follow her meaning, but she knew she would stay until they let her take Davos home. It took Officer Palau more than half an hour to explain that he could not go home with her unless Dr. Steinroe said he could. But when Dr. Steinroe came back into the office, she shook her head and tried to reassure Lily that the best thing for Davos would be a few days under observation. Dr. Steinroe seemed very understanding at first, but as Lily held back, she began to become more assertive. "My signature is needed for him to go home, and I will not sign anything until I have a much closer look. He seems right now to be a very disturbed boy. I don't want him out where he can hurt himself." Lily protested, then began to weep.

Mr. Cisneros took Lily home. There was no question of her coming back to school for the rest of the week. He made that plain to her. He wanted to help her straighten things out before she returned to her classroom. He began to talk about how he understood this kind of thing, but before he could go into detail, drawing on examples from other schools he had worked in, she put her hand on his arm to silence him. She needed quiet. She needed to think.

Lily spent a lonely evening. She sat in one place fighting against the tears. At first she thought she could eat nothing, but by the time the evening news came on she had heated up the leftovers she had planned for her and Davos. She ate praying that there would be no mention of Davos and her agony. Luckily, a shooting at the Ala Moana Center resulted in a standoff between the police and two men who barricaded themselves in the Payless Shoe store with several employees. That took up almost all the news because the negotiations were broadcast live.

In the silent house, Lily sensed her fear rising. The evening had grown dark quickly. She cleaned the dishes and turned the lights on in the first floor rooms. Upstairs, she turned the lights on in her bedroom and then stood for at least a full minute in front of Davos's door. She wanted to go into his room, but she hesitated. She had always made it a rule to respect his space. That way you would not lose your child to repressed anger. That policy almost guaranteed early maturity. She always knocked first and waited for Davos to invite her in when she had to talk with him. Now, with him gone, she did not know what to do. In a fit of instinct, she knocked on his door, waited a few seconds, then went in. Everything was immaculate. He had made his bed with hospital corners. His school books sat on the chair in front of his desk. On the desk Davos had positioned a notebook open to a blank page. His chess set balanced on a pedestal against the wall, with all the pieces standing ready for combat. His CDs filled the two cases he had built under his boombox. They were alphabetical by artist. In the two low book cases he organized his books alphabetically by author and in the cases in which there were more than one book by a single author, he alphabetized them by title as well. All the photographs on top of the bookcases faced toward the south wall so that, as he studied the chess board he could see them.

From the ceiling he hung his model planes, beginning with the largest plane, so they all flew uniformly from the east to the west, although Davos had not built a model plane since he was sixteen. Lily took great pride in his neatness, but she carefully avoided overpraising him for it. Mothers could spoil things if they were not careful.

She sat at his desk and touched his notebook. At first she did no more than run her fingers lightly over its cover. It was like a diary, not something you would want anyone else to read, but it did not say "Diary" on its cover, like the diary she had when she was a girl. So perhaps it was all right to open it. She needed to understand as much as possible about Davos's state of mind–not that she didn't truly understand him. Didn't she overhear him telling Marnie Sanders that his mother was the only one who truly understood him? And at that thought, she opened the notebook and began to read. The first pages were filled with chess notation, games he had played and written down for later study. The first part of the notebook had a divider, and she quickly saw that everything in that section was devoted to chess. She turned to the next divider and saw that he had copied out some lines from plays. She did not recognize any of them, but they seemed serious and they were certainly interesting.

The last section of the notebook had pages that were dated and recent. Davos's poetry filled these pages. Lily knew that he wrote poetry, but he had never let her read any of it. It was private. She knew he read poetry only because she had overheard him reading some to Marnie over the phone early in the school year. She could not hear what it was about. All she heard were the rhythms and the pleasant sounds and then she heard Davos tell Marnie that he had written them. She turned to the last page and read.

Blister white and make it red
Angels come to soothe the dead
Their hair is dark and subtly curled
Because of grief throughout the world

31

When my Angel offers peace
Then the troubles Lord will cease
Take my self and shake it so
I am the Angels that I know
Their voices keep my body free
When Angels come and measure me
They say I've got a mission goal
To make the shattered pieces whole
Everything is sacrificed
The way it was with Jesus Christ
Disorder rules the world at large
And Angel voices give the charge
Now I know that I was sent
The Angel of Supermanagement.

Lily studied the poem and read it over several times. She was surprised that Davos did not use commas or periods. She was also at a total loss to understand what Davos had written. But like many people she never could understand poetry. It surprised her most that Davos had written the poem so neatly, and without any erasures or additions. The poem was dated today. He must have written it before he went to school.

She turned back a few pages, but the earlier poems appeared to be nonsense. A few made sense, but they were simple, four-line verses about love and death. They were easy to understand and certainly seemed ordinary enough. She closed the notebook and stood up. His closet door had a movie poster of John Travolta, something he'd put up just after school began. She hesitated again, but slid the door aside and saw that Davos had all his jeans together, then his dress trousers, then his shirts, then his two nice jackets. Next to them she saw two capes. One was maroon, the other yellow. She knew that Davos had the capes, but she always thought they had something to do with the plays he was in. She closed the door and began weeping.

Dr. Steinroe would not let Lily Caceres see her son. She called her early in the morning to explain that she had ordered Davos kept for observation and that she would talk with Davos again later that day and if they could work things out, she would see Lily then and try to help her understand what had happened at the parking lot on Beretainia Street. Until then all Lily could do was to sit tight and not worry. "Not worry?"

"Yes, don't worry. It won't do any good. I'll talk with Davos and see where we go from here, but there is absolutely nothing you can do. He's safe and he seems calm."

"When can I see him?

"When I say so, and I can't say anything until the end of the week."

When Dr. Steinroe finally called her, Davos had been in the Kapiolani Center for eight days. "I need to see Davos." Lily had become frantic with worry.

"You need to see me first." And with that, Lily went to Dr. Steinroe's office in an untidy rambling Victorian building that seemed to house nothing but doctors. Dr. Steinroe was on the second floor and the sign on her door said to knock and then wait in the hall. Lily twisted her fingers in front of the door and tried to stifle her fears. Finally the door opened and Dr. Steinroe, wearing a black dress with beige ruffles at her wrists, ushered her in. Dozens of folders sat on one side of her desk, on the other were several large books, some open, some closed. The telephone sat on the floor, and beside the desk several towering piles of books and papers threatened to fall at any moment. When Lily sat down she saw that a half-empty box of tissues lay near her elbow.

"Davos is a very sick boy." Dr. Steinroe brushed something off her chair, pulled it out roughly and swiveled it toward Lily. As she sat she rifled through the folders to her right and selected one for attention. "Tell me a little about his homelife. How has he been feeling lately? Have you been worried about him at all?"

That was when Lily had to tell her about the divorce, how Davos's father simply did not understand him and how he had run around with women from the hotels when he should have been working and how Lily finally put her foot down and took charge of her life. Dr. Steinroe simply stared at her. "What was Davos's relationship with his father?"

"I'm not sure he cared."

"His father?"

"No, Davos. I'm not sure he cared. His father never took him places, never read to him, never did the things you'd expect a father to do. He never even learned how to play chess with Davos. And Davos, as I'm sure he's told you, loves chess more than anything."

"He didn't say."

"His father's name is Noa. He lives in Kahuku. He's a building superintendent. He sees Davos probably three or four times a year. No more."

"Have you noticed any strange behavior in Davos?"

"Pardon me?"

"He's in a dream world. I'm sure it's been going on for a while."

"My God. It hasn't been going on at all. He's fine. He was just fine the morning that all this happened."

Dr. Steinroe wrote something on the third page of the folder. "I just hope you understand it's hard for me to believe you haven't noticed anything. Did you know that he says he is an angel? Has he ever said this to you?"

"You must be wrong. This can't be true. He's just pushing himself too hard. This is not a crazy boy. He's such a leader."

Dr. Steinroe held up her hand for Lily to stop. She was very abrupt. Her hair was disordered and her glasses sat above her ears reflecting the flourescent ceiling light. "Please, stop all that." Dr. Steinroe stopped and seemed to struggle to remain patient. She took the folder and placed it in the center of her desk, then turned again to Lily. "He's had what you would call a breakdown. Now, I know that's difficult to hear. You would call it a nervous breakdown, but actually we don't know yet exactly what that means. I'm not going to tell you we can pinpoint this, because we can't. It may be something he will have to live with under medication, or it may be something that will pass in time. Either way we must make sure we do exactly the right thing for him. We haven't done the entire workup yet, but by the end of the week I'll have a report from two other psychiatrists who are also looking at him. Dr. Jane Koto and Dr. Hyam Jameison, both with a good deal of experience. You'll have to stop crying if we are going to get anything done here today. As I was saying, Davos is resting right now. He's communicating and that much is good. But what he's experienced does not come out of the blue. This is something that has been going on."

Lily was stunned. Nervous breakdown. There was never any mental disease in her family. She wondered about Noa's side. She only knew a few of his relatives, and while they were a bit odd, there was nothing to suggest they were crazy. Noa himself was stolid, but by no means out of the ordinary. What had happened? Was there something she had done while she was pregnant? Some trauma at birth? What? Davos was a wonderful boy. How could this woman tell her he was crazy?

"He's on medication right now. I think we may have found a good balance, but you know how these things go. You have to keep right on top of it and adjust the medications as necessary. This is going to take a lot of getting used to. You're going to have to change the way you live."

This woman was missing the point. Davos did not need medication. He needed someone to take care of him. Lily felt guilty that she had been so involved in the Menehune fete lately and had stayed after school much too often. But that would stop.

"I haven't seen him in days."

"I'm not sure it's a good idea to see him now."

"But I'm his mother." Lily drew a tissue from the box. "I'm his mother. I want to do the right thing."

"Of course, of course. Can you wait until the morning? I assure you he is in no danger, and he is not distressed. I asked him directly if he wanted to see you or his father and he told me that his true parents are in heaven and that he had no parents here."

Lily almost burst into sobs, but she held on. How could Davos say that? They had dinner every evening. They saw each other at breakfast. She looked away from Dr. Steinroe and held the tissue to her face.

The halls gleamed in the Kapiolani Center and the odors were like balsam. They were the odors of health. Dr. Steinroe was eleven minutes late and seemed more distracted than even the first time Lily had met her. She took Lily into a small sitting room with a large picture window that looked out on a patch of drooping sandalwood leaves. The sun reflected from the walls opposite.

"He will be here in a minute. I want you to be calm."

"Calm? I haven't seen my son for more than a week and you want me to be calm?"

"For his sake. He's on heavy medication. Haldol. It's important that we not upset him."

Lily knew she would not upset Davos. If anything, he would be upset at not seeing her. Would he think she didn't care, that she didn't want to see him? Was he feeling guilty about what he had done and did he think she did not forgive him? Of course she forgave him.

36

When the door opened Davos shuffled in wearing a crinkly white jumpsuit and noisy slippers. He walked so slowly that Lily was shocked. He never lifted his feet and the sound was like that of an old man in a geriatric ward. She stood and took a step toward him and he stopped. For an instant she thought he might turn and leave. But he began moving toward the other side of the table. Lily went to him before Dr. Steinroe could get between them and she put her arms around Davos. She told him she loved him and missed him and as she spoke Davos stood still and hardly said a word. She heard "Mom," and "Okay," but little more. Davos had a small notebook in his hand and when Lily let him go he moved ahead to the chair and sat down. He began to rock gently in the chair. When she sat in front of him, she saw that he was heavy-lidded, that his lips were dry and cracked and that there seemed to be white powder in the corners of his mouth. He seemed unable to focus. She asked him how they were treating him and whether he could sleep well in the hospital and he simply nodded as if every question could be answered by yes. Lily looked to Dr. Steinroe.

"What has happened to him?"

"He's gone through a very bad experience and the medications are the only thing holding him together right now. You have to realize that he must stay on his medications until I see him in two weeks. It's going to be up to you now."

"You mean I can take him home?"

"Of course. That's why I wanted you to wait until now, when I can release him. He's been stable like this for three days and I am sure he won't be a problem."

"Davos is not a problem." Lily reached for his hand, but he did not stir. He seemed not to see anyone in the room. "Oh, my sweet Davos. You can come home."

Dr. Steinroe gave Lily a bag of medications with detailed instructions printed on each box. She had to start each day with the proper meds in the proper order. Then make sure that Davos followed up with another cocktail of medications at night. Lily had brought Davos's clothes–the ones he had left in the locker room at the supermarket–and gave them to Dr. Steinroe, who called an attendant and instructed him to get Davos ready for his release. While he dressed, Dr. Steinroe said that she thought he had done very well.

"What will happen?"

"Happen? I can't tell you. The medications will help until I see him, then we will step them back until I get exactly the right mix. But you cannot expect too much." She stopped for a moment to engage Lily's eyes. "It's possible, I don't like to say it, but possible that Davos may never be himself again."

Lily simply could not absorb that message. Of course he would be himself. He was himself. What did this woman mean?

"I don't want to alarm you, but we need to watch him closely. If he shows signs of a quick recovery . . . ." As she spoke, Davos shuffled out dressed now like a person. His face was slack. His eyes seemed unseeing. She tried to smile at him, but she feared it might look false. She took his arm and held the medications and her purse in her other hand and steered him toward the door.

"Okay," she said. "My office. Two weeks. And good luck. You've got my number."

The first week was very difficult for Lily and Davos. Davos hid in his room and came out only for meals, and sometimes she feared he might not come out for those. She knocked on his door the first evening he was home and waited for Davos to tell her to come in. But he did not. Finally, she opened the door and spoke his name. He sat in front of his chess table arranging each piece so it was in the exact center of its square. This seemed to take a great deal of concentration. Davos looked up at her and smiled. It thrilled Lily to see a recognizable emotion on his face and she struggled to control herself.

"Are you feeling better?"

"E5 answered by B6." He smiled again and moved two of the pieces. He positioned each exactly in the center of its square with such precision and care that Lily had a sense of admiration for his skill. He looked up at her with a kindness in his expression. "Caro-Kann," he told her. "Angels approve of Caro-Kann."

She had no idea what he meant.

"The bishop," he explained. Then, in an intimate voice, "Is really an angel of insurrection."

"Are you an angel today?"

"Of course. Don't you see?"

Lily realized he wore his cape over his white shirt. She had not noticed it.

"The world is coming apart. You can see that. Fissures. It's drying like a pomegranate and will split soon along the lines of the fissures. That's when I can help most. People are disorganized. That is a sin that the angels do not forgive." He went back to his chess board and moved a white piece, then a black piece. It took him some time to place them exactly in the center of each of their squares.

"Pomegranate," he said once more, looking at her with a calm, beatific expression.

The next day in the market she stopped and looked at a pomegranate, but decided to buy a mango. She thought of making chutney. The manager came to her while she balanced a mango in each hand and asked after Davos.

"Fine, he's doing very well."

The manager expressed concern and told her he hoped Davos would come back next summer for his old job. She smiled at him.

But when she came home she saw Davos on the floor of the living room on his knees straightening out the long fringe on the short side of the oriental rug she had inherited from her mother. He was confounded by the reluctance of the fringe to stay straight. He would stretch the threads and they would soon curl slightly and he would go back to them and then move on again.

She knew enough not to stop him by saying it did not matter whether the fringe was straight or curled, so as she went into the kitchen she just said quietly, "I need some help putting things away." She knew that Davos enjoyed putting groceries away and after a few minutes he left the rug and began to organize the cans of soup, the tuna fish, the beans, the chili, and the boxes of pasta. When he was finished all the cans faced outward, the pasta was in regular order, and he sighed.

By the end of the first week Davos seemed to be more relaxed, more communicative. But on that Friday night he frightened her terribly. She woke suddenly and saw him looking down at her out of the darkness. His face was placid and almost sweet looking. He straightened her bedspread and told her very frankly that he had spoken with the angel and the angel had made him feel happy for the first time in many days. He then turned and walked back to his room. Lily sat up in the dark for more than an hour wondering just what he had experienced.

Within two months he was back in school on a reduced load. He was driven in a sedan with two other young people and delivered home by an aide who walked him to his door and made sure he went inside. He went to school for only four hours each day and when he was told that his part in the play had been given to someone else he simply smiled and explained that he had an interview with an angel that would take several months and that he was relieved that he would not disappoint anyone by staying home to meet his angelic obligations.

Lily had read about angels in the Bible. But she decided to keep quiet when Davos tried to explain how the angels spoke to him.

Whatever they talked about, Davos always seemed oddly fulfilled afterward. He said they were reassuring talks and that the angels had a mission for him because he was one of them. After such conversations, she made sure that Davos really had taken his medications. Fortunately, he seemed to accept Dr. Steinroe's directions and kept to the regimen she prescribed. From what she could tell Davos liked Dr. Steinroe much more than Lily did.

Davos's progress heartened Lily. Three months after the episode Dr. Steinroe had cut back the medication twice but warned Lily to watch for any recurrence of hallucinations. Davos appeared more himself. The flush in his face–and the attendant puffiness–had disappeared. Some of his friends called the house for him in the evening and sometimes he spoke with them. He still spent time straightening the fringe of the living room rug, but when Lily entered the room he would stand and smile and begin to explain how Lily could save time by creating a small daily planner in which she scheduled all the important activities she needed to do in any given day. Davos gave her a sample page that he had printed up on his computer. He had scheduled her rising, her ablutions, her breakfast, and her preparations for leaving for school, her hourly schedule in classes, including lunch, which he must have gotten from Mr. Cisneros, her return to home, her preparation of dinner, her television time, especially the six pm news, and her bath and even her bathroom time. At first, she thought Davos was very thoughtful and she thanked him. But it did not take long for her to realize that Davos had prepared such schedules for a number of his friends, showing them how to take advantage of wasted time and how to be sure that they actually accomplished all the tasks they had set out for themselves.

Mr. Cisneros showed her the schedule Davos had worked up for him. He left space for student conferences, meetings, teacher conferences, assembly, and after school monitoring. "If I followed his schedule," he said with a smile, "I would probably be able to go home early. Lord."

But outside school one afternoon, Lily was stopped by Marnie Sanders. "I can't do all this," she said, giving Lily a small sheaf of papers. Each page was a scheduled day. "If there's any way you can tell him." Lily did not quite understand. Then she looked at the schedules and saw they were precise down to ten and fifteen minute intervals. Lily wanted to ask her if she was still Davos's girlfriend. Or just his friend. She didn't know what she meant exactly, but she knew she was searching the girl's face for a sign that she thought Davos was normal.

Lily's anxiety tapered off through the summer. Davos organized himself in such a way that he was able to make up some of his classes in summer school, so there was still a chance that he might be able to go to the University in the fall even if he only took one or two classes. Lily tried not to snoop, but she watched Davos very carefully. He was taking his medications, she was fairly sure. But he did not seem as bright and happy looking as she had hoped he would. He seemed to have forgotten about the disordered rug in the living room and he sometimes moved his chess pieces with what almost seemed a sense of abandon.

One of his classmates at Molokai School agreed to be one of his roommates in Moana Hall at the University. It was a relief to Lily. Davos seemed excited at the prospect of being on his own and some of the old Davos began to show up in his conversations, which were a bit more assured, more focused and less volatile than they had been a few months before. Dr. Steinroe had once explained to her that these kinds of breakdowns were unpredictable. And she said they took many forms. It was entirely possible that Davos's episode would never repeat itself. If Davos could stay well and avoid stress he might be able to live without any recurrence at all.

The house without Davos felt strange at first, but soon she

understood what being at peace with herself really meant. She had been "walking on eggs," as one of her neighbors described it, and now she could come into her living room and not fear that something terrible had happened while she was away or that Davos might have retreated into a place where he could not be reached. They still had planned meetings with Dr. Steinroe, but they were months, not weeks, apart. Lily was suddenly grateful when she and other classroom teachers gathered to discuss this year's Menehune fete and things seemed to have returned to normal.

But things were not normal. She learned of Davos's death from her former husband, Noa, who had been called by the University in the middle of a bright October night. Noa was so abusive on the phone that she could not understand what had happened. He blamed her for spoiling "the kid" so that he was good for nothing. "How could he be a man the way you babied him? Jesus, you drove him crazy just the way you would have driven me crazy if I'd have stayed with you. You bitch you." Shaking, hardly aware of herself, Lily cut him off and called the number she had for the university and found that Noa was right. Davos had killed himself running through a glass window in his dormitory. His roommate had tried to stop him, but Davos was much too big and much too fast.

"He put his arms out," his roommate told her when Lily came to campus and tried to gather Davos's things. She knew she looked like a broken woman and she felt like a broken woman. "I think he thought he could fly. He kept saying crazy things, tried to get me to clean up the room like it was some big deal, and then he got dressed in his cape and we were all having a floor party and he must've done drugs or something because he was definitely high. I've never seen anyone that high."

When Lily finally brought Davos's things home Mr. Cisneros came over to offer her some solace. He tried to tell her how it was not her fault, how these things happened, and once again Lily stopped him before he could finish his sentence.

"I don't know. But I think he died happy," she said.

Mr. Cisneros seemed puzzled.

She pulled out a box and stood some medicine bottles on the table between them. "He took these with him to school, his new medications. He never opened them. He was so sad when he took his medications. He told me how much he missed talking with the angels. He was an angel, he said. And now I think I understand what he meant. He had too much to organize when he went away. The world was too large for him. Much too large."

A View of the Ocean

When Lawrence Tanaka's father died in Germany in 1944, his mother Lucia took in boarders as a way of making do, and because she had many relatives in Poi'pu and Lihue she knew she would not starve. Mama Gretchen came down from Lihue to live with Lucia and her children and freed Lucia to go back to work. Times were difficult, but eventually people came back to the island and business began to thrive again. After Lawrence finished school, he worked in Pearl Harbor as a welder, but his constitution was not up to the job and he took sick and had to come home. His mother collapsed that year and it turned out to be lung cancer. She was still young and attractive. With his sister Nele grown and married and living in Hilo with her first child, Lawrence nursed his mother with help from the Health Center. Lucia died peacefully in her rocking chair looking out at the ocean during a long September afternoon.

Nele sold him her interest in their parents' house. It was an old-fashioned low-slung bungalow with a tin roof and a small porch. But it had an ocean view at the bottom of Poi'pu at Sunset Kahili. When he was a child during the war, Lawrence spent his mornings scouring the sea for Civil Defense. Twice he knew he saw submarines surface at dusk, but when he told the Air Raid Warden, Tom Whiston, nothing happened. Tom Whiston, himself only a teenager at that time, came down to the house and walked along the ridge with Lawrence looking out at the water and said only that it must have been humpback whales. It was the right season and they were about the same size as submarines.

When the war was over, Lawrence and Tom surfed together

in the early mornings. Tom had his own board built by one of the Kamehana brothers at Nukaumoi beach. Lawrence used his father's old board during the winter, when the waters at Sunset Kahili were mild and gentle. Later, after Tom began work in Lihue, he lent Lawrence his board and Lawrence hitched rides in the summer months up to Hanalei where he surfed the big waters. He never reached the heights of Little Bobby Kamehana, who was already a legend and about the same age, but he rode his board out as far as he wanted to go, and those mornings when school was just a memory he sat on Tom Whiston's board with the water swelling beneath his thighs like a lover. When the big waves began their curl, his heart raced and his mind soared and he felt himself swept into the torrent with the power and grace of the golden dolphins who sometimes surfed along with him.

After his mother died, Lawrence worked in a garage in Koloa. He understood engines well enough to tell people if a valve was sticking or if a rod was bent and in danger of being thrown. He knew when a distributor cap had become porous and needed to be sealed with a clear coat of lacquer. "Moisture was your enemy," he often told customers. But he was at his best when an automobile needed some spot welding. He had been well trained at Pearl and he liked to show off his skill. By the time he was in his mid thirties, he had saved enough money so that he could buy out Ben Stillman, and he wound up owning the Esso station all by himself. That was when Camille Ishigura drove in with a bad water pump. Her little Ford rolled in blowing steam through the hood and frightened her to death. Lawrence helped her out of the car, calmed her down, and told her he'd have it fixed in no time. Which is exactly what he did. But he also had a chance to talk with her, letting her know he owned the place, which meant more to her than he realized. And happily, she agreed to let him take her to lunch that following Sunday.

Lawrence had been around enough to make sure he was

46

shaved properly and that his hair hung just over his forehead the way he knew the girls liked it. He degreased his fingernails and used some pumice on his knuckles to help make him as presentable as he could. "You look real good," Camille said. When she smiled he knew he felt something that was brand new.

Camille moved in with him after a brief, but emotional ceremony at the tiny Church of the Holy Ghost in Hanapepe and began immediately cleaning and reorganizing the house. She brought her clothes with her and a few pieces of furniture that she had been given by her mother. Lawrence wanted to go to Waimea Canyon for their honeymoon. He had hiked the Kokee trails in some of the most spectacular canyon haunts and knew a spot at the Kumuwela Lookout where they could pitch their tent and be undisturbed in a paradise filled with birdsong and the music of the canyon wind. He had once seen the large golden mamo soaring lazily deep in the canyon. He told Camille about the gallinule, who sang softly in the evening as darkness fell. He made the lookout sound so romantic that Camille eventually gave in and spent a listless week searching the skies and canyon peaks for birds she had never heard of and never actually saw.

But once back in Poi'pu, Camille directed her energies to making the house her own while Lawrence worked in the gas station. Their lives changed once when their daughter Lucy was born. And when she was twelve their lives changed again. In early 1967, Standard Oil decided that the station in Koloa was not profitable and they withdrew their pumps, leaving Lawrence with a business that began dying from the moment the Exxon trucks turned back up toward Lihue.

He thought the Chevron people showed up as his savior, but quite the opposite. They explained that the station interested them, but that it was dingy and in need of total replacement. The question was simple: would he sell the place to them or did they need to purchase the lot on the opposite corner and build a new station.

Lawrence sold. And for a while he was happy not having to work. Camille was smart about money and showed him how they could invest the money and use the interest to live on. He had learned how to manage his books and how to price his services well enough so that the station had always provided them with a decent living. But the kinds of things Camille explained were beyond him. He was happy to turn the finances over to her and let her dole out the weekly money he needed to enjoy life.

Camille took a job in a clothing shop in Koloa when Lucy went to high school and left Lawrence alone through much of the day. At first, he thought he might try hiking in the canyon again, but he found himself winded and sore after only a few hours wandering down off the road onto the Nualolo Trail, which he had once hiked easily when he was fifteen. He announced that he was going to rent a sailboat and sail around the Na Pali coast and Camille smiled. "You be careful and don't go alone." He took her advice and brought Tom Whiston, now fifty years old, but always a good sailor. Tom was enthralled at the idea and set out with great enthusiasm. The weather was fine and the wind difficult, but not as frightening as it sometimes was. Tom Whiston gave him some good pointers and took the helm when the wind threatened to thrust them landward onto the rocks. It was a good day.

But Lawrence could not spend his life like a tourist. He stood looking out to sea the way he had as a child, and occasionally he spotted a whale sounding the depths. He thought of the submarines he saw as a child–he knew they were not whales. The sea was bristling and the sky, even with the clouds settling on the horizon, was much as it was when his mother was alive.

For a while, Lawrence decided that he would focus his attention on the house. The outside needed a coat of paint, so he told Camille this was the week to get the house painted. He got out the ladders and the paint brushes that had stiffened up in the shed and got to work scraping down the windowsills. Camille chose the color, a lavender that she often wore when they went to Lihue or to Hanapepe to visit Nele and her husband. Lawrence liked it and spent several weeks slowly scraping, cleaning, and painting. The house looked good and he knew it would weather well for a few more years. But eventually he turned his attention to another project: his collection of old cars.

Lawrence saw people drive by the house sometimes and slow down to look at his cars. When the Chevron people took his station, he moved the old cars he had always meant to fix and took them home. He had a '52 Studebaker, a '49 Packard convertible without its top, a Panhard that, like the Studebaker, you couldn't tell whether it was going or coming, a pale green '53 Ford Victoria, a '41 Lincoln Zephyr that had taken some bullets from a Zero in its trunk at Pearl, and a '49 creamy tan Cadillac with modest tailfins and no wheels. The grass had grown up around them as well as around the several engine blocks and spare parts that stood alongside the house. The big thing, he told Camille, was which one to start with.

"Maybe you should give 'em away," she said. The cars had never bothered her, although she knew they bothered other people along their street. One of the women in Swanson's Dress Shop commented to Mrs. Swanson about the "auto-slum" down in Poi'pu, and Camille knew she meant her house, but that kind of talk just made her laugh. The cars were Lawrence's concern, and she knew sooner or later he'd get to do something with his "treasures."

By the time Lawrence had the Packard running well, the house needed to be painted again. Lucy had divorced and moved to Honolulu and became something she called an aesthetician in a hotel on Waikiki. Lawrence and Camille visited her in her small apartment on Ainekea Way, up near the canal. She had made it look very nice and Lucy explained that she belonged to the Holy Covenant Church and they had picnics once a month and that there were some nice

49

young men who regularly came along and made life interesting.

So it was that in 1986 a man came to the front of the house dressed in white trousers, a red Aloha shirt, and a white peaked cap. He was red-faced, smiling, squinting into the sun when he stood outside the house and looked up at Lawrence. "Aloha," the man said with a smile.

"Hi."

"Whatch' ya workin' on?"

"This here's a Lincoln Zephyr."

"You're kidding."

Lawrence looked at him. He was a heavy-set man about fifty-five, round-faced, wearing a baseball cap with initials, "JDC." He looked like he had been walking a bit, but Lawrence realized he'd driven up in a metallic bronze Corvette parked on the other side of the street. Lawrence had not noticed the car and realized he'd been seriously concentrating on how he was going to get the Lincoln down off the blocks now that he'd put wheels on it and had pumped up the tires. There was a lot of rust on the undercarriage, but he'd sprayed it with rust oil and saw that he had a spare for the broken spring on the rear passenger side. Otherwise, this car needed just some new paint and new upholstery and maybe it would run pretty good when he got done.

"My dad had a Zephyr back in New Jersey. All through the war. Sweet running car, I remember."

"You like cars?"

"Yeah, I like cars. When they run." He laughed. "Best bumper sticker I ever saw was on an old Jaguar XKE. Said, "But when it runs." He laughed again.

Lawrence stood up and wiped his hands. He could see this man was not one of the Evangelicals. He didn't have a sheaf of giveaways and he wasn't wearing a black suit. Lawrence watched the man ease himself a little closer and he began to wonder what he wanted.

"Got a nice spot here," the man said after a minute. He squinted into the sun.

"Yeah."

"Oh, I didn't say my name. Martin Wren. I'm one of the real estate folks down in Lihue, the Wren Agency?" Lawrence finished wiping his hands and reached out to shake. "Thanks, I just wanted to talk to you about your place, see what you planned to do with it."

When Lawrence tried to explain the conversation to Camille, he realized he didn't quite understand everything the man had to say.

"He wants us to sell the house?" Camille said.

"Says we can get a good price if we wanted to sell."

"Why would we want to sell?"

"You said the house was a little small for us. Even with Lucy gone. This Mr. Wren says we could get a good enough price so we could go to the north shore and have a bigger place. He knows some good buys up there and wouldn't charge us a fee."

"No fee? Hmm."

Tom Whiston dropped in later that month and told Camille and Lawrence that he was moving to the north shore near the new development in Princeville. "Princeville?" Camille said in surprise. "They say that's pretty expensive."

"Got a lot of money for the old place just when I was wondering what I was going to do, whether I was really able to get it in the shape it should be or not. I sold out and got them to give me a little place set back from the water up there. I thought you both sold too."

But they hadn't. Camille figured it all out very quickly. This Mr. Wren represented a development outfit building a resort condominium hotel in Poi'pu. She'd heard a rumor in the dress shop but hadn't paid much attention to it. "They want our place," she said.

"I know, but I like it here."

"That's not the important thing." Lawrence waited for her to continue. "What's important is what they'll pay us for the place. Look at it. We can see the ocean and that's what people want. They want to see the water. Don't ask me what it is about people, but the ocean view is a big deal." Camille found a map of Poi'pu and stretched it on the kitchen table. She put an X through each house that had been sold around them. There were six other houses all positioned so that a developer could build a large complex and take advantage of the ocean. But the problem was that they really needed the Tanaka house to make the project complete.

Camille told Lawrence they were going to sell, but not for the price Mr. Wren suggested. She explained that if Tom Whiston could make the kind of deal he made, that they could do a lot better. She smiled at Lawrence. "This is our chance to be smart," she said.

When Mr. Wren sat down with them, he had a map of the proposed development. He explained that his company really had enough property to build the kind of place they saw in the artist's rendering, but that they wanted to be fair and include the Tanaka property to make the project truly complete and honor the memory of Lawrence's parents. But he also said several times that the offering price was fair and the company was prepared to build around the Tanakas if they had to. He said he felt a little sorry for them because they could make a really good profit here if only they would take advantage of the offer.

After Mr. Wren left for what he said was "the last time," Camille sat down and asked Lawrence if he knew where he could get some more old cars that didn't run. Lawrence was surprised at first, but then he saw what she meant. "Sure," he said. "Up at Breen's. He's got a lot of scrap up there. I could get a bunch of cars."

"Get two," Camille said. "Rusty ones."

That week Lawrence went up to Kini Breen's and had him haul down two old Buicks that had busted windshields and lots of body rot. Breen wasn't sure what Lawrence wanted with the old wrecks, but he didn't ask questions. Lawrence had him place them up closer to the road than his other cars and thanked him as he left. He had stopped work on the Lincoln Zephyr some while ago and started to wonder if he could get the Cadillac running. It was a straight eight, a big engine, and if it would come back to life he knew it would be a smooth running honey. It had that old pre-war manual shift on the steering wheel and would look impressive on Highway 56 up near Anahola. Except for the wheels. Then, when he went to pay for the two wrecked Buicks he decided he ought to search out some cool old time wire wheels. Kini tried to pawn a set off on him that he knew were for a Mercury, but Lawrence pressed him and after a while Kini "remembered" a set he had put aside in the shed behind his own garage. They walked over there and Kini opened it with a flourish and rooted around in the back until he tossed out a pretty impressive rim. "I got another three of these," he said, and Lawrence knew he was going to pay whatever Kini asked.

The Buicks sat in the front yard for more than a month before anyone from the resort project came back. Lawrence tinkered with the Cadillac and actually got the motor running and realized that the speedometer, which measured only 48,728 miles was probably accurate. The muffler was rusted out, of course, and the brakes would have to be completely replaced, but the important thing was that this car was going to run again. Camille was at work when he got it running, so all he could do was say a simple mahalo to whatever god it was that looked after old cars.

This time the people from the resort made an appointment. A man telephoned the house and Lawrence turned it over to Camille. She agreed to a meeting at a restaurant near the airport in Lihue. When she and Lawrence arrived there were three men and a woman, all dressed in dark suits with ties. They had chosen a large round table near a window off to the side of the restaurant so they could talk and not be disturbed. It was clear from the first that these people had just flown in and would fly out again when their talk was done.

"We've reviewed the work that Mr. Wren did with you and we wanted to go over a few things. I think you know what we have planned for your area of Poi'pu." With that the tall man gestured to the blonde woman and had her give Camille and Lawrence two large brochures filled with colorful pictures of well-off people around a pool watching their children play with inflatable animals and pink beach balls. Around them were plantings such as Camille and Lawrence had never seen in Poi'pu, and beyond them were exotic sand-colored buildings. "You can see that what we have here is a dream, but a realizable dream. The Poi'pu Resorts will complement the beauty of the south shore as few projects ever could. And we want you to be part of it."

"We like things as they are," Camille said. She smoothed her dark hair and smiled directly at the talking man.

"Yes, we know that. But what we are saying is that you will like it even better when you understand what we are offering."

"It would have to be very, very good," she said, knowing that now she admitted these people would eventually get what they wanted.

Lawrence was proud of Camille. The deal was vastly better than he could have expected. They gave the Tanakas three times their original offer. They also gave them a place on the north shore in Princeville as they had done for Tom Whiston. But with a condition. There were to be no automobiles visible anywhere on the property. They would have a three car garage as long as they signed a contract and covenant guaranteeing that they would keep the grounds clean of rubble or garbage or cars. And finally, because the Poi'pu Resorts was a condominium complex with time shares, Camille demanded they be made owners of a two-week share. She explained that Lawrence and she enjoyed the ocean view and would like to return to it for a small portion of each year. Shockingly, none of the four representatives seemed surprised, and all were obviously relieved when Camille and Lawrence shook hands and walked away with a folder of signed documents changing their lives.

Camille decided she could quit her job and for a while both she and Lawrence were in the house throughout the day. They spent their time putting things into boxes and getting ready to move. And once Lawrence's things were ready, he realized he had some major decisions to make about his collection of cars. He had decided early on that he would keep the Cadillac and let the other cars go. He called Kini Breen and told him he could have the Buicks back and that there were a few other cars that he wanted towed away. The Lincoln Zephyr sold the first week it was in the paper and Lawrence watched it driving away up toward Koloa, thinking that the amount of money he got for it was small consolation for letting such a car go. But Camille had helped balance things by deciding that they would buy new cars, a Toyota Avalon and a nice new Honda Accord. That left one garage and one car, the Cadillac.

The Whistons, like the Tanakas, had a new two bedroom home up close to highway 56, far from the new clubhouse and the brilliant hotel. They were almost segregated. The other houses near them were condominiums owned by people they never saw. But among the few people in Princeville with whom they spoke, Camille found a friend in Connie Toshi, a woman who married the golf pro at the Prince golf course.

Tom Whiston talked Lawrence into playing some golf. Lawrence never thought of playing golf himself. That was a haole sport, he thought, but he also realized that with some haole blood of his own, he might just as well try. He went with Tom to the pro shop and bought some new clothes, a new golf hat with "Ping" written on it, and new shoes with spikes that made a grating sound on the asphalt outside. His dark red pants and his club tee shirt made him

55

look like the other golfers he sometimes saw standing on the course leaning on their clubs.

"You just hit this ball, right?" he said, holding the Titleist 4 that Tom had given him.

"Sure, and we can play as long as it's not on the weekends. That was part of the deal. So it'd be stupid not to play. They won't let us play on the Makai course, but this one's just as good I hear."

So Lawrence and Tom went into Lihue and found some golf clubs and bags at Costco and showed up ready to play on a Tuesday morning. They had to wait for a half hour or so, and when they were ready to go out they didn't realize they had to use golf carts in order to keep the traffic moving on the course. Both Tom and Lawrence came back a bit confused when the boy stopped them from walking after their tee shot.

"I'm real sorry," Lawrence told the boy who brought them over to the carts. They had already paid for the cart without knowing it.

The boy had to come out to them again twenty minutes later when they were searching in the rough for their respective Titleists. They had lost track of their shots and time as well, and the boy had to explain that people were waiting to tee off after them. "Sorry," Lawrence said. He looked around at four people with pastel shirts and dark hats waving. He waved back.

They lost their first shots, and after that they struggled through the next two holes with one ball–Tom's– in a water hazard, and another–Lawrence's– in a bunker where he drove it so deep into the sand that he had to pick it up and throw it on the green. By the time they reached the seventh hole neither had any Titlests left, so they had to bring their carts back to the clubhouse and give up. They went in and had a cold beer and sat talking with a knowledgeable old timer named Jimmy Kamehana who offered to go out with them on another day and explain some of the protocol. He used that word, and

Tom Whiston asked him how come no one told them about the protocol. Jimmy laughed. "Oh, everybody here figures you come out to play golf you know what's what. You know how it is with these folks."

"They can play golf, then I can play golf," Lawrence said. "It's in the agreement."

Tom Whiston nodded. "My first game," he said. "I guess you gotta get used to it."

Jimmy Kamehana took them out the following week, winning three dollars a hole from each of them every time they played. "Cost of living," Lawrence said when he and Tom walked back after their last game. "Cost of the education. My mother always said that. Learn the hard way is the best way."

"Jimmy showed us how. It's only fair, I guess. We pay him something."

"You think we can learn this thing?"

"Golf? Jeez, Lawrence. We're already in the swing. What else you gonna do?"

And that was the problem.

They lived in brand new houses and the sun was the same sun they saw in Poi'pu, but the ocean was not the same. Lawrence sometimes went near the water and looked down on the whitecaps, then looked out to the open ocean. He never saw the whales he enjoyed down at Sunset Kahili. He never saw a school of dolphins. It was not the same.

"You need something to do," Camille told him. "The ocean is the ocean. Besides, we can go down to Poi'pu for our two weeks later in January. You'll see. Things be much better then." Camille seemed to make the adjustment very easily. She spent some of her time in Honolulu with Lucy and she even accompanied her to the Holy Covenant Church and sang in the Sunday choir. Lawrence drew the line at church. "You go," he said. Church was okay, but it wasn't for him.

When he couldn't play golf, he worked on his Cadillac. Now with the spiffy wire wheels and the whitewall tires he got from the Sears catalog, it was beginning to look good. He used Bondo to fix some rot and some irregularities around the passenger side door, then applied some primer to keep everything together and saw that it was going to cut quite a figure when he got it out on the road.

Lawrence worked slowly and carefully. Sometimes Tom Whiston stopped in and they had a beer while they talked about the south shore and the way the sun hit the water at sunrise late in the year. Tom didn't miss the old place as much as Lawrence did, although he agreed that there was really no comparison. "But," Tom said with a sharp look in his eye, "look at what they gave us. This place is a palace, right? And the way they keep the grass and the landscaping. We don't have to do a thing. And it's brand new. We got some deal, Lawrence. We got some deal."

One night in late October, Lawrence got the Cadillac running and Tom Whiston followed him in the dark up to Kini Breen's to have it prepared for a paint job.

"You gotta do this right," Lawrence told Kini.

"Shit, you know I do this right."

"I don't know. I saw what you did for that kid Kolo with the Volvo."

"Piece of shit, that Volvo. Never make that car look like anything. No, I make this a beauty for you. Then you get Sammy the Norwegian to do the upholstery and you got yourself a real car here."

Tom Whiston watched this exchange in the harsh fluorescent lighting of Kini's large service bays. The Cadillac looked menacing, humpbacked, and distressed. Tom had never been in Kini Breen's. He'd heard about him from some people at work, how he might be involved with some stolen cars one time–of course, that might have been just vicious gossip. But he did know that Kini Breen had a reputation for being a badass drunk and turning seriously violent when he was crossed. But Lawrence seemed to know how to handle him. Kini talked like someone building up to a brawl, saying every word with emphasis, and speaking very, very loud. It was his way, Tom guessed, but it didn't phase Lawrence. Lawrence slowly explained just how he wanted the car to look when it was finished. He had the paint shipped in from a specialty house in Detroit called Classic Paintz, so he was confident it would be authentic looking and make the car gleam.

Lawrence went back two days later and watched Kini's boys mask the windows, lights, and chrome. He told them to take their time, which they did. And at the end of the week the first coat of that creamy light tan he liked so much hid all its speckles and patches and made the car suddenly look as if it had come onstage in an old gangster movie. Kini's boys set up the red heat lamps to cure it and Lawrence went home in his Honda a happy man.

Tom helped Lawrence pick the car up, again at night, and drive it slowly back to Princeville. He explained that he didn't want to drive too fast, just in case he might pick up some debris in the breeze. The paint job was very good, as Kini promised, but it wasn't completely set. A stray stone, a low-flying bat, even a large moth could do damage at this point, so it was smart to drive carefully.

When the paint was another week or two set, he took the car down to Sammy the Norwegian's for examination. The interior headliner was wrecked, like most of the flooring and the front bench seat. The rear seat was soiled, but mostly in one piece. The doors needed everything new. Sammy knew Lawrence was coming and had the catalog of interiors set out for him to examine. Together they chose the classic burnt sienna interior and Sammy said it might take three weeks for delivery.

It took two months. While he waited, Lawrence played golf several times with Tom. Tom was getting better, but Lawrence seemed to be about as bad as he was that first day. He never got through nine holes without losing at least two golf balls. He let Jimmy Kamehana tutor him on his swing enough so that he thought he might look at least respectable even though he wasn't really hitting the ball very well. When he told Tom that he had 147 on the day, he joked and said it was good because it meant he really got a lot of use out of the course. But he also noticed that sometimes when he teed off the group behind him would laugh. They didn't laugh out loud, not enough to make him turn around, but he could hear the snickers. And when he was behind a group he would watch these tall haole address the ball and with a profound "whack" send it out of sight so fast that he could not follow it. They moved with assurance and, yes, even with grace as they mounted their carts and zoomed after their shot. It made him wonder if he would ever learn to love the game now that he had time to play.

On one of the most discouraging golf days Camille and her friend Connie Toshi came to play with Lawrence and Tom and played so well and with so much enjoyment that Lawrence wondered if he should ever go out on the golf course again. Camille broke a hundred and Connie Toshi was angry because she shot an 88. Lawrence just said he didn't keep count, but he knew that he was still shooting over 130 and had little hope of improving. Tom Whiston was also humbled by the experience even though he said nothing. He hid his hangdog expression behind a beer while Lawrence bought the women mixed drinks with little umbrellas.

Camille enjoyed herself and spent so much time with her friends that Lawrence had time to put the final touches on his Cadillac. Sammy the Norwegian had some trouble with the fabrics that were supposed to be close to original for the '49 Cadillac, but eventually he found a way to make the tucks and the turns that were essential to making the car look like new. He fixed the headliner in a masterful fashion and made the doors look new. He sprayed the inside of the car so it smelled much as it had when it came from the showroom.

Lawrence would not let Sammy drive it to his home. He told him firmly on the telephone that there was no question but that he would do the honors himself. The car, when he saw it, was parked at an angle in front of Sammy's garage.

"Didn't I tell you?" Sammy said proudly.

"Wow," Lawrence said, touching the creamy tan paint of the passenger door. The interior was indeed just like new. He bent over and looked in the front and back.

"Sit in it. I did the springs over. I didn't just cover that old crap in there. I did a job. You're gonna love it."

"I love it already. It's lookin' good."

"Radio's a little weird. Lots of static."

"It's only AM," Lawrence told him. "That's how they were then. But we still got AM stations. No problem." He paid Sammy and drove the Cadillac out onto Highway 56 and slowly toured down with the ocean on his left. He had the windows open and the wind touseled his hair. He had a smile on his face. He took the car all the way to Poi'pu and then motored on to Sunset Kahili to see the construction of the Poi'pu Resort. He had to admit that it looked beautiful. The new plants and trees, the flowering hedges and the fountains impressed him with their elegance and expense. Nothing remained of his old home. At first he was not even certain where it had been in relation to the new buildings. He stopped at the head of the drive leading down into the Resort itself. He saw three young men in the turn-around looking up at him, expecting him to come down the drive. But he did not. He paused, then drove back to Koloa and parked in front of the post office. He really just wanted to park the car and see if anyone would notice. When he came out of the post office with three stamped postcards, he saw two men standing in front of his car pointing to the grille and the hood ornament.

"Great car," one of the men said. "I used to love these when

I was a kid."

"You wanna sell?" the other man asked.

Lawrence just laughed. He touched the roof by the driver's side. "Can't sell this baby."

Lawrence gassed up in his old station, now serviced by Hess Oil. He checked the oil himself and was a little disturbed to see it was down a bit. He realized it could be an oil burner, but what did it matter? A little oil was nothing. He lowered the hood and heard the satisfying chunk as it slammed closed. What a car. When their two week stay rolled around, Lawrence proudly drove Camille and their luggage down to the Resort and blanched when a local boy he'd seen grow up nearby took the door of his car and held out his hand to help Lawrence out. At first, he resisted valet parking, but Camille just brushed it off with a smile and pointed to their bags. Lawrence stood there for a moment and watched his car drive off and around the corner out of sight.

Their apartment's bedrooms flanked a large living room. One bedroom had a walk-in closet and a jacuzzi. The kitchen's espresso machine and microwave oven surprised Lawrence. But Camille told him the only meal they'd eat there might be breakfast and maybe some evening coffee because she was eating out.

That first afternoon Camille got into her new bathing suit, put on her sun hat and sat by the pool in a shady spot. Lawrence brought the paper with him. He would not swim in a little pool like that. He swam in the ocean. What did people want with swimming in a pool with lots of kids screaming and adults just floating around stupidly? Lawrence examined the people around the pool. Most of them were getting a bad sunburn. While he looked around he realized that the condo they had put them in was almost exactly where their old house had been.

"Our condo is it, isn't it?" he asked Camille.

She had been stretched out and almost asleep. "What?"

"Isn't that where our house was? Right here."

Camille sat up and blinked her eyes. "Where? Here?" She looked back at their condo, then around toward the pool. There were no landmarks to help her. An old mango tree with a hollowed out trunk had always stood behind the house as a landmark when she drove home, but no mango trees remained in the new complex. She stood up to look out at the ocean, but her view was blocked by the other buildings ringing the pools. All she had to go by was the sun. "I think you could be right. Maybe a bit further back, but more or less. So what?"

"Nothing. I was just thinking. You go swim."

"Ruin my hair?" She laughed and stretched out again to snooze.

The Resort obliterated his family home. They redirected the road outside the Resort, and inside the buildings stood on separate levels with flowered walkways and lights shining up into the trees. The plash of the fountains confused him when he tried to get his bearings. He agreed with Camille that they had a decent condo here at the Resort and that the view was almost the same as when they lived there. But the way the other units restricted their sight-lines made Lawrence feel cheated. The Resort's intention was to frame the view of the ocean, but Lawrence did not need a frame. He liked the ocean the way it used to be.

Camille seemed unaware of the Resort's changes, but Lawrence grew more and more annoyed. He walked along the Resort's seawall overlooking the ocean. They left no way down to the water except for a spot where they provided a few chairs and a warning on the pebble beach. Lawrence ignored the warning one morning, borrowed one of the surfboards stacked nearby, and paddled out to where he could look back to study the low-roofed buildings clinging to the high ground. The light made the buildings glow. From the water there was no sign of any of the houses that once were on Sunset Kahili.

A few people said hello when he and Camille dined in the Resort restaurant, but they said little more. He tried talking with some of the men in the early evenings when the Resort provided free drinks and free pretzels on the verandah. But they just smiled and usually hid behind the stock reports in their evening papers. Camille talked cheerfully to the women they met, most of whom came with children or with old friends who gathered together and usually left her out of the conversation. After a while she stopped talking.

Lawrence learned the daily schedule of the cable shows and watched reruns of *Jeopardy* and *The Dukes of Hazard* and *Mayberry R.F.D.* while Camille sat by the pool reading. He dozed in the afternoons with the air conditioning revved at high even though the ocean breezes cooled their small outdoor sitting area. He wanted his money's worth. At night Lawrence took the Cadillac out on the Poi'pu road searching for a restaurant. Some of their old haunts remained in Koloa, but Camille needed to check out the other resorts. He was happiest when some of the exiting diners gathered around his car and started pointing out details they remembered from their youth. "Neat car," they'd usually say. And laugh. Lawrence would laugh in return. A touch of joy. "Looks like new."

Both Lawrence and Camille drove silently back to the north shore after their two weeks were up. The Cadillac hummed loudly and Lawrence stopped at Kini Breen's to have the oil checked and to listen to Kini bellowing proudly about his paint job. "Look at this baby, you look at her. Such a job we done. How you like it?" Camille smiled politely. "Sure you like it. Man, how could you not like it? Gotta a classic car there is what you got. Shit, look at those wheels. Those the wheels I sold you? Man!"

Just hearing his voice made Lawrence feel better.

Tom Whiston showed up the next morning while Lawrence was in his robe having coffee on his small patio. "How's about a ride?"

Lawrence looked at him.

"'Member? You promised me a ride when you got the interior done. I tell you, it looks so good I can't believe it."

When Lawrence got himself ready and into the car, Tom slid in next to him and touched the dashboard and the headliner as if he were looking for flaws. "Incredible," he said

Out on the highway, with the windows open and the sunlight bathing the road, Tom asked him about the Resorts. He hadn't bargained for a time share at the Resorts himself, so he wanted to know what it was like.

"Great," Lawrence told him.

"I haven't been down to see it."

"It's great. Terrific."

"Nice rooms?"

"Sure. Big living room and TV."

"People treat you okay?"

"Oh yeah."

"Ocean view?"

"Yeah. Perfect," he said, pulling the Cadillac into a rest stop in Hanalei where they could stare out at the young surfers idling in the water, waiting for the first perfect wave of the day.

Having Lost

O n his first morning in Honolulu, Percy Hefferman planned to take a taxi to the shuttle for the Arizona Memorial at Pearl Harbor. He read all about it in the Airline Magazine on the leg over from Los Angeles. The Memorial was essentially a bridge straddling the Arizona, hovering over the water without touching a bit of the gigantic battleship. You could look down into the front of the sunken ship and then walk to the other side and peer down into the rear, where more than eleven hundred American sailors were still entombed.

Percy was neither warlike, nor especially patriotic. He was in ROTC in college because they paid most of his way through, but after his four years in Germany babysitting a great deal of electronic equipment–a job that eventually led him into setting up his appliance store–he was finished with the military. And although he did not picket or walk around any campuses with placards, he basically thought the Vietnam War was as much of a mess as anything the nation had ever gotten into. If he had had a draftable son he would have told him to go to Canada and wait things out. One of his best friends sent his son off to Sweden in December 1967, just about the time the blood ran thick on the evening news and Lyndon Johnson explained how we would win the war. Only two months after that, Percy's nephew, Cooper, his sister's oldest son, was declared missing during the Tet Offensive. It was pretty obvious that he had been killed somewhere outside the American Embassy in Saigon during the heavy fighting there, but for some reason his body was never found. A number of American GI's had been killed and burned with tires around their neck so the bodies couldn't be identified. Percy thought Cooper was one of those, but he never said a word to his sister, who held onto hope for several years. She never gave up until the embassy fell to the Vietcong in 1975. Percy watched the evacuation on television and knew he was right about the war from the very first. Why couldn't the politicians figure out how to let the army do its work? Why couldn't they keep their nose out of impossible situations. The French had been stupid in Vietnam, but that was the French. From his months in Saarbrucken and Frieburg, he had begun to understand a little about the French.

But there was something more pure, more honorable in that other defeat, Pearl Harbor. The sneak attack, the deception, the feckless political maneuvering in Washington. The article in the airline magazine had reviewed the details for him, and he realized that when brave men face impossible odds and nonetheless stand fast that people should take note and do them honor. So he knew that he had to make the pilgrimage and pay his respects, even though that terrible morning had taken place almost a decade before he was born. It didn't matter. He knew what his obligations were.

Ideally, he wanted Lisa, his wife, to come along, but she was not interested, and especially not interested in trying to make the 8:30 am shuttle. She turned over and grunted softly when he came back from showering and brushing his teeth. He closed the door softly and waited for the sluggish elevator. Being on the thirty-sixth floor had its advantages: no bugs, a nice view of Diamond Head, and a partial vista of Waikiki, for what it was worth. But the disadvantage was apparent when the elevator was still not there after a four minute wait. He checked his watch again. He'd have to get a cab and he'd seen no cabs when they went out for dinner last night. But there had to be cabs in Honolulu. He must have seen them and not realized they were there.

The desk clerk called a cab from the stand only a block away and Percy was in plenty of time for the shuttle. He tipped the driver, a dark man named Irisawa Isibura, or something like that. The celluloid protector for his licence was scuffed and not entirely clear. His picture was blurry, too, and for a moment he thought that maybe the cabby was an impostor. But no. He was a middle aged man, thoughtful, serious, unsmiling. He held out his hand and Percy gave him the fare and a tip, which the cabby took with a nod and zoomed off. Percy stood watching the Chevrolet turn around and head back to town empty.

He entered the shoreline Visitors Center and got his ticket for the next tour. The man who led the talk was a Pearl Harbor survivor who had been on the Nevada when it beached itself under heavy fire outside the harbor. He tried to explain how his skipper had tried to get out to sea so as to avoid the worst of the attack, but on his way out he saw that if they were to get hit any harder the ship would completely close down the harbor, so he beached her and had his men concentrate on shooting down as many Zeros as they could. As the survivor admitted, that was not very many. The battleship was not well designed for dealing with swarms of fighters.

The survivor, who was named Ray, according to his engraved tag, was a stooped man, shorter than Percy, and he spoke slowly. There was little trace of emotion in his voice, which told Percy he had given this talk many times. He explained how the Japanese planes had come from landside and shocked everyone with their bombs and their machine gun fire. But the real terror, he said, came from the torpedoes they let loose in the crowded harbor. His best friends all died that morning, and he said something about how it was the end of innocence, a phrase that Percy knew was concocted for the tourists, but still a curious twist in the conversation of a man who seemed to be reliving, at least for a moment, some of the experience. The hall was filled with tourists, many of them Japanese, only a few of whom could have remembered the bombing of Pearl. Most of the people listening to the survivor were younger than Percy and some of them seemed a bit impatient listening to Ray, whose speech was that of an old man: slow, filled with pauses, and sometimes a bit uncertain. When Ray finished, a dapper Japanese man moved forward and said a few words in Japanese. The Japanese tourists laughed, but politely. Then the Japanese guide made a number of gestures that seemed connected to the events that had happened at Pearl Harbor and seemed to be repeating much that Ray had explained. Percy caught words for the Nevada, the Utah, the West Virginia, the Arizona, the California, and several other ships that he could not make out. The Japanese man pointed to photographs of several Japanese carriers and apparently described the way in which the attack was mounted. Percy wished he could understand what the man was saying.

When the lecturing ended, some people stared again at photographs familiar in documentaries on the History Channel. The Arizona in flames, the Oklahoma upside down in the water, the Nevada drenched with raining bombs and diving Zeros. The twenty-three minute film retold the story of the surprise raid both in English and in Japanese, an irony that he had not quite been prepared for. He imagined that if the Japanese had won the war there might also be a Memorial, but he was quite sure that the accompanying videos would have been presented only in Japanese. When the film was over, the Navy launch arrived to take everyone out to the Memorial.

The boat filled quickly. He saw quite a few young families with two and three children, all revved up, making noise, posturing dangerously near the openings in the railings on the deck. Percy found the coffee bar inside and he made his way in for a Danish and a regular coffee, some semblance of a breakfast. He took his coffee out to the front of the boat and listened to the excited children screaming, demanding information, shoving each other, and twirling their baseball caps at odd angles. A scant few of the passengers were older men, white-haired, wearing caps brocaded with the names of warships and the numbers of squadrons. Percy imagined them paying tribute to fallen comrades.

He studied one tall red-faced man with a dark blue double-breasted blazer with sparkling bronze buttons. He wore a snap-brim hat and a pair of dark sunglasses that made him look like an official, although he had no name plate, no obvious identifier. It was odd to see a man dressed so formally in Honolulu–or at least so he thought. Percy had been in town only for an evening and part of a morning, so he could be quite wrong, but he thought, from what little he saw of the people in the airport, that Hawaiian-shirt casual was the order of the day. However, this man was aristocratic in a yacht-club way. And he was tall and forceful looking, with a shock of stark white hair beneath his hat.

Behind him Percy saw several Japanese families swarming onto the boat with a rising sound of gabble. The parents were very young, younger than he thought parents usually were. They were also short and relatively thin. Their clothing seemed mildly outdated. The women's dark skirts were long and flared slightly at the bottom. The men wore short sleeve dress shirts. Some of them had pencils or glasses in their shirt pocket. Their children dove aboard loud, rambunctious, and joyful in their gesticulations. The Japanese children he had seen in Teaneck were very well behaved, quiet, and serious, not like these kids. This batch was clearly different.

Another large group of Japanese adults arrived almost immediately afterward and Percy saw that they seemed all to know one another. The young woman leading them stopped by the launch and gave them a brief talk in Japanese. Percy could not understand a word, and when the group mounted the steps to his level he heard them talking softly with one another. He imagined they were being reverent, considering that they were visiting an important war Memorial, but he could not be sure. He looked over at the man in the blue blazer, but he seemed deep in thought, leaning on the railing, looking down into the water.

Once under way, the children ran into the snack bar and out again with bottles of soda and snacks. Some of them had to be restrained when they showed signs of running along the deck or when they seemed about to toss a bottle over the side. Percy knew he had little tolerance for misbehaving children, but he tried to be resilient. He knew that nothing he could say to these children would have slowed them down for a moment. Nothing he could say to their parents would make any difference. So he decided to be stoic and self-controlled. The sight of the first memorials low to the water took him by surprise. This was "Battleship Row" and all the floating memorials had ships sunk beneath them. So many.

When he finally saw the stark white Arizona Memorial he felt a surge of emotion. The structure resembled a boat, although more upside down than rightside up. He wondered why its seven large window-like openings were coffin-shaped. The breeze filled the flag masterfully, and a sense of pride overcame him as they drew closer to the dock. For an instant he seemed in a world by himself. The children and the tourists melted away and he felt almost alone staring at the gravesite of so many heroic men. And then the laughter of a teenage Japanese girl broke through his revery. She was right next to him and she poked at a boy almost her age. He poked her back and they ran down the deck in screels of laughter as the boat pulled into its berth.

Percy stood still while the boat docked and the tourists flocked to the gate. He waited while they went down the gangway. When he saw the man in the blazer begin to make his way to the exit, Percy moved along near him. This man had some dignity and Percy felt a sense of comaraderie with him. The Japanese tourists had already reached the dock and began walking through the doorway to the Memorial. What Percy had not realized was that the deck below had also filled up with many more tourists, most of whom were Japanese. For a moment, as he was moved along in the throng, he wondered just what a Japanese tourist made of a Memorial for sailors that their own nation had killed. What would have gone through their mind?

Most of the Japanese tourists huddled together in the Entry Room while their tour leader explained what they were looking at. What would that leader have been saying? Percy stood with the group and watched the slender young woman with long, supple black hair and large lovely eyes telling people–what? That December 7, 1941, was a day that would live in infamy? He thought not. Would she have told them that their people planned a massive sneak attack and virtually destroyed the U. S. Pacific fleet? He didn't think so. Instead, he imagined that she was telling them how their nation, with its back forced to the wall by the imperialistic tendencies of American industry's progress in Pacific markets, had done the only honorable thing. They had struck back. But would they really believe such a story? The serene looks on their faces told him they experienced neither guilt nor regret. No, he realized that for these people, this was an historical tourist attraction, something like a wax museum, although partly submerged.

Percy followed a few people into the Assembly Room and watched as several women moved to the huge portals that looked like windows when the launch approached the Memorial. The sun was low overhead and the sky scudded with clouds. It may have been just such a perfect day in that long ago December. He looked up to see a commercial skyliner rising from the airport heading west. When he approached the portal to look down into the murky depths where the Arizona lay, he saw several people toss their leis into the water with a sense of reverence that gave him pause. He could have brought his own lei here instead of storing it in the refrigerator with Lisa's. If only he had known. After a few minutes, the water beneath him was strewn with flowers.

When the Japanese tourists came in with their leader they also threw some leis into the water. The adults were very serious in their expressions as they moved through the Assembly Room and positioned themselves to look through the openings into the water. The Memorial straddled the Arizona in the midships so that one could peer into the main body of the ship from two directions. He heard people speaking in quiet tones, but communicating, pointing to portions of the ship, explaining things. The Japanese children felt some of the seriousness of their parents and seemed subdued. The man in the blue blazer stood several portals away, but he too was grim faced and serious.

Percy moved up and to the other side and realized he was not going to be able to get to look directly down at the ship until the tourists in front of him vacated their positions. Two short Japanese women threw some flowers into the water, a gesture that reassured him. But when they turned to move back, two Japanese boys, about eleven or twelve–it was hard to tell–took their places and one of them dropped a full bottle of soda into the water with a sound that indicated he was "bombing" the ship. He and his friend smirked, then laughed aloud. With a swooping motion, the boy's father took his arm and snatched him away, speaking firmly in Japanese as he took him back to the Entry Room. When Percy looked down, the soda bottle had risen back to the surface and bobbed slowly as it drifted shoreward.

"Did you see that?" Percy said to the man in the blazer.

"I'm sorry?"

"What that boy did?"

"With the soda bottle?"

"Yes. A disgrace."

The man looked at him closely. "You know what they say. Boys will be boys."

"I know, but here. To do that. After they saw the film."

"Probably gave them the idea."

"I think it's symptomatic."

"Of what?"

Percy was not sure. "Well, of discourtesy I suppose. This is supposed to be hallowed ground. Isn't that what the man at the Visitor Center told us?"

"I don't think those boys understood English."

"Someone should have told them in Japanese."

"They did. It didn't help. They're kids."

"Maybe you're right. I suppose it's too tempting. I guess they just don't know what this place means to us."

The man nodded and crossed his arms.

"This is my first time in Hawaii," Percy said. "How about you?"

"I live here."

"In Honolulu?"

"Yes."

"You come here often?"

"My father's down there." He nodded toward the forward hold.

"My God." Percy hardly knew what to say. "There are more than a thousand men down there, aren't there?"

"Some were found and removed, but most of them are there. I've come out here every once in a while since the Memorial was opened in '62. I used to take the tourist boat, but this is easier." He began to move away. "I hope you have a good time while you are here."

Percy turned and looked down into the water, down into the gigantic ship. The flowers and the bottle had drifted out of sight. He studied the turrets, the decking, the huge fittings. And then he turned and moved into the Shrine Room. Many of the tourists were already there reading the names on the wall. Here at least there was a hushed silence as if this were somehow a cathedral. All those names, all those dead, all those men beneath their feet. He got close enough to begin reading:

HAVERFIELD, James Wallace	ENS
HAVINS, Harvey Linfille	S1c
HAWKINS, Russell Dean	SM3c
HAYES, John Doran	BM1c
HAYES, Kenneth Merle	F1c
HAYNES, Curtis James	QM2c
HAYS, William Henry	SK3c
HAZDOVAC, Jack Claudius	S1c
HEAD, Frank Bernard	CYA
HEATER, Verrel Roy	S1c
HEATH, Alfred Grant	S1c
HEBEL, Robert Lee	SM3c
HECKENDORN, Warren Guy	S1c
HEDGER, Jess Laxton	S1c
HEDRICK, Paul Henry	BM1c
HEELY, Leo Shinn	S2c
HEIDT, Edward Joseph	F1c
HEIDT, Wesley John	MM2c
HELM, Merritt Cameron	S1c

Was one of these the father of the man in the blazer? Percy looked around to see if the man was nearby, but he was not. He apparently had walked back to the Entry Room.

Percy looked up at the towering wall covered with names incised in marble as if this were the nation's tombstone. He feared for a moment that he might weep. He realized his face was flushed and his eyes moist. The films of his youth came back to him, especially "From Here to Eternity," his first Pearl Harbor flick. He turned his face toward the wall and closed his eyes for a moment to regain his poise. When he turned back he realized he was in the midst of the crowd.

The Japanese families paused for only a moment or two before the wall, as if they were there just to verify that the number of dead was huge. He doubted that the words meant very much to them. The children stood near their parents and stared up at the names for a moment, then turned back and headed toward the Assembly Room where they could look out into the harbor and study the movement of ships and the sounds of airplanes overhead.

When he walked slowly back to the Entry Room, Percy saw the man in the blazer approach the Japanese guide he had seen earlier. She was a beautiful woman wearing a smart purple Hawaiian shirt and a short skirt. The man in the blazer spoke to her in Japanese, "Ohayoo gozaimasu"* She smiled at him and touched his arm, "Konnichi wa,"* she said, and laughed. They exchanged a few more words, then switched to English. Percy had the impression that the young woman worked for him. He couldn't be sure because they walked on and turned from him, but it seemed from the way she deferred to him, that she was an employee. Neither went back on the shuttle to the Visitors Center and Percy remained puzzled. The fact that the aristocratic looking gentleman spoke Japanese surprised him. But what also surprised him was that the emotional swell he had felt so strongly in the Shrine Room had melted away once he was on the shuttle. He looked back at the Memorial and realized that he was hungry. It was lunchtime.

On shore he called Lisa and suggested they meet at the Princess Kalulani for lunch. Lisa took a few minutes to study her map and when she found it told him that she had wanted to go to the International Market Place anyway to get some Hawaiian shirts for gifts. Percy's cab dropped him off on Duke's Lane by the side entrance to the Market Place. Percy walked in through a display of garish Hawaiian shirts that he could never have thought of giving to friends, much less wearing them. Because he was fifteen minutes early and Lisa was always fifteen minutes late, he took the escalator upstairs and wandered through the open air walkways. He realized that virtually every public place in Honolulu was open to the air.

* *Good morning.* **Hello.*

76

The temperature varied by only a few degrees year round, and it rarely rained. That was why the Memorial Assembly Room had an open roof and no glass in the portals over the Arizona.

He stood for a moment in front of a show window looking in at extremely large paintings of sea and surf. Some of the paintings were ghostlike, evening scenes that were probably intended to imply some rich spirituality connected with the sky and ocean. He stood there only a moment or two when an older white-haired Japanese man dressed in a light linen suit and tie touched his arm.

The man bowed slightly. He hesitated a moment looking at Percy. "Sumimasen,"* he said.

"I'm sorry, I don't speak Japanese."

"Having lost," the man said, gesturing with his hand. "Having lost."

It took a moment, but Percy realized the man was lost. "Okay," he said, nodding his head. I think I understand what you mean. You're lost." He said the last word very distinctly.

The man smiled at him. "Outriggle Leef wa doko desuka?"* Percy was puzzled.

"Outriggle Leef," the man said again, holding out a card.

Percy took the card and studied it. When he put on his reading glasses he saw the card was in Japanese. However, on the other side he saw the name of the hotel: the Outrigger Reef.

"Ah," he said, "Outrigger Reef."

The man smiled and nodded vigorously. "Having lost."

"Okay, Okay. Let's get the map." He took out his hotel map and brought the Japanese man over to the light. He put the map down on the horizontal surface of the wall looking down on Kalakua Avenue. He took out his pen and placed an X at the spot where they now stood. "Here," Percy said. "We are here right now. Here." He gestured broadly to indicate his meaning and the man seemed to

* *Excuse me.*   * *Where is The Outrigger Reef?*

77

understand.

The man pointed to the floor at his feet and said, "Heal. Koko."* After a second he repeated, "Koko."

"Koko," Percy said, also pointing to the floor. Then he took his pen and drew a dotted line southward and westward until it ended at the Outrigger Reef Hotel, right on Waikiki Beach. "There," Percy said, marking it with a large X and pointing in the direction indicated by the map. "The Outrigger Reef is there."

"There," the man said. "Soko, soko,"* he said, touching the X and then pointing in the proper direction.

"Soko," Percy said, hoping he was being helpful. "Here, take my map." He smiled at the man, who bowed graciously and thanked him in English.

He took the map and backed away toward the escalator. "No lrost," he said, smiling, and began downstairs. Percy leaned on the cement and watched as the man exited the Market Place and reached the street. The man turned and looked back. He pointed westward and Percy nodded. "No lrost," the man said loud enough for him to hear and stepped off briskly.

Lisa was seated at a bright, lovely table in the Princess Kalulani's dining room. The bustling restaurant was virtually full of happy looking, healthy people in bright floral colors. Lisa put the large menu down when he arrived.

"Did you have a wonderful time?" she asked.

Percy thought for a moment that she might have been sarcastic. But after a second he realized he was wrong.

"Interesting, an interesting time."

"Did you weep?"

He smiled at her. "What do you mean?"

"Oh I know you," she said smiling brightly. "The flag overhead, the boat in the water, patriotic music. You're easy."

*Here. * There.

"Ship," he said.

"Ship?"

"Yes, it's not a boat in the water. It's a ship. A battleship."

"Oh yes, I should have remembered."

"And I learned a little Japanese. Koko soko."

"What's it mean?"

"God only knows, but it's Japanese. Around here you've got to speak Japanese. At the Memorial that's about all they spoke. Japanese. Can you believe it? I think everybody in Hawaii speaks Japanese."

"Well," she said happily, "I suppose we'll have to learn. But after lunch. I'm famished."

Volcanic Jesus

The squall drove in from the east with a heavy wind swirling the water upward through the vestry window until Martin Lahiri rose to secure it back into place. The old windows needed a great deal of maintenance, although it was only when the roar from the bending koa trees became deafening that they truly caught his attention. Martin had poured all his concentration into the sermon for next Sunday, when he had promised to say something about the nature of evil and God's role in its creation. He had sat at his old ormolu desk for more than an hour thumbing through his Bible without coming to any conclusions that he thought the congregation might be able to accept, much less understand.

He went back to his desk and thought for a few minutes more, considering the comments that Auntie Violet had made about how God must have created evil and if so why would anyone want to worship such a God. Auntie Violet had been problematic over the years, and Martin–who had been named for St. Martin de Poris, whose dark skin matched his own–knew enough not to counter her directly. He watched the Toshis and the Mahanamoas at the coffee sharing hour, when people brought honey cakes and fruit breads for the great table, to see if they reacted to Auntie Violet. They seemed to dismiss her as mad and did not notice the import of her comments. But Martin knew that Auntie Violet enjoyed posing conundrums. She grew especially virulent regarding the nature of the trinity, and Martin had dispelled doubts about the trinity in more than a dozen sermons spread over a decade. Nothing, however, satisfied Auntie Violet, who always seemed resourceful beyond his expectations. She would remain dormant for months on end, only to rise in the most unexpected moments of profound inquiry and pose impossible questions.

As he sat there reflecting on his response, the window flew open again and flapped wildly until he rose and pressed it closed. The outside light changed dramatically as he held the window closed and watched the rain sweep down its surface. He saw the image imperfectly when the light changed again as a cloud scudded by. At first it was vague, strangely vague. He took off his glasses and looked around for a Kleenex to dry them. The moisture had blurred his vision, just as his hours of labor had dulled his sensibilities.

He found the Kleenex in the bathroom, where he decided to wash his hands with soap and to rub each lens clean of its accumulated oils and grime. With perfectly clean glasses, he stepped back into the vestry and stared at the window. The image was definitely there. He stepped behind the desk to get a different view. Still there. At the doorway he studied the window and saw that the image had become more distinct, more clearly there. How could this be? He had lived with that window for eighteen years, since he had moved over from Ala Moana in the east Honolulu vicariate, since he celebrated his forty-fifth year in the priesthood. He had never seen anything in it before. He rarely looked at it, and when he did he merely looked through it. That's what you did with windows. But now he could not argue with what he saw. It was faint, but distinct: an image of Christ. It was much like His image on the Shroud of Turin, a long, sad face whose eyes were closed and peaceful.

Martin knew it had to be his imagination. This could not be a genuine image–in the sense that it was a miraculous manifestation. It must be a figment. He rubbed his eyes and sat at his desk. After a moment he rested his head on his hands and began to doze off. Mrs. Manalato woke him with his late afternoon tea and he realized he had been asleep for more than an hour.

"The rain was good for the garden," Mrs. Manalato told him. "The roses, too. Are you all right?"

"I guess I dozed for a minute. I'm fine." He watched her to see if she looked at the window, but she just went about laying the tea and cookies out as she always did. She did not glance in the direction of the window. When she left he turned and saw that now with the sun out the image was easily visible. Anyone who looked at the window would see it clearly.

He followed Mrs. Manalato back to the kitchen.

"Would you have something like a pillowcase, Mrs. Manaloto?"

She looked at him. It was an odd request. She seemed to stifle a comment. "How many do you need?"

"Just one."

Back in the vestry he took some pushpins and stood on the sturdiest chair and covered the window with the worn pillowcase so that it resembled a curtain. It was only a temporary fix. When he finished and got off the chair Mrs. Manaloto was standing in the doorway.

"Do you want a proper curtain?"

"No, no. It's just temporary. Disturbing my concentration."

"Daylight?"

"A glint," he said. He wanted her out of the room.

"A glint, eh? Glints disturb concentration?"

"I said, it's temporary."

She waited at the doorway as if he were going to deepen the conversation with some kind of revelation, and when he remained silent at his desk she eventually left. She did not study the window, nor did she appear curious. He turned and looked again at the window and saw the image behind the pillowcase. It must be his imagination.

He stood up and went to the doorway. Again, the image was

there, faint, but absolutely there. After a moment he closed the door and went slowly upstairs to his room and found the hand mirror he used to inspect his bald spot. Downstairs, with his back to the window he held the mirror in front of his face and studied the window. The image was definitely there, definitely the image of Christ. Indeed, it was all the more impressive in reverse. Suddenly, he realized that if it were visible in the mirror that it might be visible outside the church. He put the mirror in a desk drawer and walked through the hallway into the nave of the church, up past the twelve pews and out the door onto the lawn. The rain had stopped and the dark clouds were moving up and over Kilauea. On the vestry side of the church he stared at the window. The image was all the more visible for his having placed the pillowcase against the inside. And from that vantage point the image was all the more convincingly similar to that of the Shroud of Turin.

Martin walked back through the church, took down the pillowcase, and returned to the lawn. Thankfully the image was less visible. He knew it was there and certainly it could be seen from the outside of the church, but now only darkly.

In the vestry, Martin closed the door and stood on the chair and studied the glass. It rippled like all old glass. The church was built in the 1860's in traditional island gothic wood style, with older windows salvaged from a church in San Mateo. Martin examined the window frame to determine his approach.

Back in the church, he studied each of the long narrow gothic arched windows. Nothing was visible in them. He walked outside with his hands behind him, trying to look like a man concentrating on his Sunday sermon just in case Mrs. Manaloto was watching him. Nothing showed up in the windows in the body of the church. The image of Christ was only in the vestry room window. Plain as day, as Mrs. Manaloto would have said. Martin took his Mercury wagon into Hilo to Kaufmann's Lumber and talked with one of Mr. Kaufmann's sons.

"You want to replace a window? You got its measurements?"

Happily, Martin had two sets of measurements. He had measured the glass area itself, then the entire window frame, which, as it turned out, was still a standard size and told Danny Kaufmann just which window pane he needed.

"I don't know how to put it in," Martin said.

Danny smiled. "We can do that for you, Father."

Martin waved him off. "No, it's time I learned."

Once he had Danny convinced, Martin listened to his instructions, backed up with a small brochure from the Lofgren Glass people. Martin paid for the glass, a chisel, a small can of putty, and a bag of glazier's pins. Danny insisted that he take a small can of white paint with him, along with a beveled paintbrush for the trim. But before he left, Danny told him once again that they'd be glad to put the window in at no additional cost. Martin smiled feebly and left.

He saw the first few cars on the church lawn before he turned into the church parking lot. They gathered on the vestry side of the church and several people stood in the bed of Ben Nagoda's new Ford pickup. Martin gasped. One of the children saw him and cried, "It's Father Martin." Once the cry went up all was lost. Martin pulled the Mercury into its parking space and closed the door behind him. "Father, come see. Come see," little Mary Kalihana said, breathless. "It's a miracle." She took his hand and led him to the vestry side of the church. Mrs. Manaloto had replaced the pillowcase that he had pointedly removed. The image was absolutely clear for anyone to see.

Ben Nagoda fell to his knees and began saying his rosary when he saw Martin. This was the most pious thing he'd ever seen Ben Nagoda do. Ben sat in the confessional once every month with tales of fights in Daggett's bar by the airport or in The Deuce in Mohouli Street near the University. Mary Kalihana, still holding his hand, looked up and said, "It's a picture of God."

Howard Kalihana came over to him and took Mary's hand. "It's a sign, Father Martin. Do you see it?"

"Yes," Martin said. "But it's not a sign."

Lila Chang heard him. "It's a miracle, Father Martin." As she spoke an Izuzu Trooper and an F-150 pulled off the road up to Volcano House out of curiosity. People clustered near the vestry window. Martin thought of the new window pane in the back of the Mercury. If he had been prepared he could have prevented this. If he had broken the window when he first noticed the image . . . . But he had hesitated. Was it blasphemy to destroy the image? Lila Chang touched his sleeve. "People will come to St. Agatha's from everywhere to see this."

"I hope not."

"They must see it," Lila Chang said.

Howard Kalihana agreed. "You gotta see this. Everybody's gotta see this. You're blessed when you see this. I was just here Sunday and I didn't notice anything in this window. Did you?"

Martin shook his head. He turned from the crowd and walked through the main door of the church through the meeting room and into the kitchen. Mrs. Manaloto was not there. He walked into the vestry room and found her looking up at the pillow case.

"I took that down on purpose."

"I thought it fell down. I wanted to help." Mrs. Manaloto was obviously shaken. "What does it mean?"

"It doesn't mean anything. It's an illusion. Something in the glass. It's old glass and something must have happened during the storm. It's a lightning print. Electrical energy, something. I have no idea what. But it does not mean anything."

"Tell them," she said, pointing toward the growing crowd. They heard the hum of the excited conversations outside. "You've got to do something."

Martin smoothed down his soutane while he thought. "Yes. You're right." He walked slowly out on the lawn and held his hand upward in a blessing. "In nomine patris," he said, hoping the Latin would give them pause. Their talk died down. "Please kneel," he said. "Say with me, Our Father Who art in Heaven . . ." and he began the Lord's prayer, which they picked up quickly. They all kneeled and chanted the prayer. He added a "Hail Mary," and when they were sufficiently quiet he began an impromptu sermon, "When our Savior walked the earth the sight of His face was a blessing beyond our capacity to understand. He conferred a beatitude such that it will be one of our rewards in heaven. If we see a shadow of that image today . . ." he turned to the window, which still showed the image plainly, "then we must claim it as a reassurance of the final day and add it to the blessings of the Lord which we already enjoy."

He heard little Mary Kalihana say "Amen" loudly enough to spur the group, still on its knees, to echo her. For an instant he thought that Mary Kalihana's face was bathed in a special light, but that would have been impossible. Besides, it would be dark in half an hour and if he could hold on he could move the group indoors to keep it from growing. Fewer cars were driving up to the caldera at this hour, and it was still possible to contain this event. But only if he were to act quickly.

"You all know Our Lord's words." He struggled to find something Christ had said that would be appropriate, but he was clearly having trouble. "'Follow me,' sayeth the Lord," he said, moving toward the doors of the church and motioning with his hands. The group, numbering something around a dozen people, slowly got to its feet and began to walk toward the church door. Only a few of them were parishioners. Others were perhaps locals, perhaps tourists. He could not be sure. Little Mary Kalihana stood by his side and took his hand as she had done earlier. He felt her gentle tug as he moved along with the group.

When they were inside, Martin stepped up to the altar and blessed the assembly. He stood before them reciting the twenty-third psalm because it was the only one he knew by heart. When he finished he smiled at them. "We have seen a taste of heaven in our little paradise. And with that in mind we must remember not to taste the apple of regret which lies in its midst." He spoke mysteriously on purpose. "What we have seen in the vestry window is not a miracle, it is a gift. A gift to us, for us, for our spiritual enrichment. My children, we are chosen for a blessing that is beyond our understanding. It may be that we do not deserve such a blessing in our hearts. Only the Lord knows what we truly deserve. But we must be very careful and help the Lord achieve what only the Lord may achieve." He raised his hand again and spoke: "'The Lord is made my fortress and my refuge, and my deliverer: and in him will I put my trust.'"

Martin stepped in front of the lectern. "What we have seen is for us only, as I have said. It is very important that you all go home and pray for forgiveness and eternal peace. But most important we must not speak of this to anyone. Anyone. Especially those who would deny us the blessings of the Lord by making us a spectacle."

"But people should share what we have seen." A woman in jeans and a halter top spoke. "If this is for real it shouldn't be hidden should it?" A tourist and probably a Protestant.

Martin smiled at her. "Bless you. Your heart is in the right place, but what I mean is that when the Lord makes His gift to the people of His church it is not for them to parade them before the world, but rather to contemplate them in the effort to understand the true nature of God, the nature clear in His manifestations."

"You don't want us to tell anyone?" the woman said.

"That's correct. All of us must hold our confidence among ourselves."

"Can I tell mommy?" Mary Kalihana asked.

"Yes, of course. But no one else. We want to keep this holy experience holy. If you tell others there will be a . . . a madness leashed upon us. We cannot have that."

"Bless us," Lila Chang said, as she slid forward to her knees.

Martin stood straight before them and intoned as he genuflected, "In the name of the Father, the Son, and the Holy Ghost, Amen."

Slowly the group rose and began to file out of the church. It had grown dark outside and Martin prayed that Mrs. Manaloto had taken down the pillow case and had not turned on the vestry room light. In the darkness the image might not be visible. When all the cars had gone and he was alone, he went outside and found his prayers answered. In the dark, he saw only a shifting range of crooked reflections on the surface of the window.

Mrs. Manaloto, who had stayed much longer than she would have done on any other Thursday, asked him what she should do. "Nothing. I mean, nothing more. You've stayed longer than I would have expected. And thank you for taking down the pillow case. Everything is fine."

"Then I'll be going, Father."

He noted the formality and nodded to her. She drove off down toward Kurtistown and when her lights were no longer visible, he went to the Mercury and took out the window pane and got his tools.

Martin heard the first voices near daybreak. He turned over in bed, aware that he strained his back wrestling with the ancient rock-hard putty. If only he could have taken the window frame out and down to where he could get purchase, he would not have had so much difficulty. As it was, he spent three hours prying loose the old nails that held the glass in the frame. He got the new glass in easily because Danny Kaufmann had given him enough trim for a good fit.

Painting it was not so easy. The soft putty sometimes yielded to the pressure of the brush, and because his hand was no longer as steady as when he was young, he used the pillowcase as a cleaning cloth, sometimes messing the glass. He was no good at such things and came close to cursing his inadequacies–were these his only ones– before he finally had the job done.

But the voices directly below him, outside the vestry room, brought him to his senses. At first they spoke quietly as if aware that Martin might be asleep in his room above them. He rose and made for the bathroom across the hall. He shaved crudely, rubbed water on his stiff gray hair and pummeled it with the fancy brush Mrs. Manaloto had given him. His eyes were puffy, and his hands speckled with paint. He used his nail brush, but could not get it all off. His questionable linen would have to do. On his way, he secured his Bible in his left hand and studied himself for a moment in the hall mirror. His shoulders stooped more than usual, and the twinge in his back made it impossible for him to do his usual military straightening before descending the stairs.

"Father Martin," the man said. He was a youth, possibly twenty-two, dark-skinned, dark-haired, enthusiastic. "The sighting. Which window is it?"

"There is no sighting," Martin said.

"But we talked with Ben Nagoda and Howard Kalihana and Lila Chang down at the Red Rooster. They saw the image of Christ without question."

"They were definite," the other man said. "They said it was like Lourdes."

"No," Martin said. "This is nothing like Lourdes. Nothing. Please, there is nothing for you to see."

"We're stringers," the second man said. "Jeff Pollitt, and I'm Jimmy Beniwa. We're with the news services, CNN, Reuters, AP. This is important news."

Martin sighed. "Please. Look around. There was a stir last evening, yes. Nothing more. I can see why people would be interested. It must have been the storm. It was a fierce storm."

"I wouldn't say that," Jimmy said. "Brief. Maybe intense."

"Unusually intense," Martin said. "Storms do odd things here on the slope of Kilauea."

"They said it was the vestry window. This is the vestry, isn't it? The right side of the church."

"I don't even know what a vestry is," Jeff Pollitt said.

"Where priests get dressed for Mass, but now it is my study and sometimes a conference room."

"May we see it?"

Martin pretended annoyance, but eventually admitted them to the vestry. They looked around for a moment, then moved to the window. Jeff Pollitt touched the frame and stared at his fourth finger for a moment. Martin prayed that the paint had dried. He slid his Bible on the desk and placed his hands out of sight in his soutane. "I don't see anything," Jimmy Beniwa said. "Do you see anything?" His friend shook his head. "Could be visible only from outside maybe."

They went back outside the church where several cars had pulled up with curiosity seekers wandering across the lawn. Three tall men and their equally tall wives sauntered across toward the vestry talking and gesturing. This was what he had feared. The newcomers began a conversation with the stringers, who pointed toward Martin. Martin felt strangely apart from the experience. He simply wanted them to go away.

"You the priest?" one of the men said.

Martin smiled at him. "Would you care to enter and pray with me?"

"God no," the man said. "No, it's just that Milly and I were up at the hotel and we heard about the Christ in the window, that he was crying and there were real tears. Which window is it?"

90

"You are welcome to come in and pray. If you'd like to take communion . . . ." But the man began walking back to his wife and the newsmen. They made some inaudible comments about Martin, then began talking animatedly among themselves.

Martin went inside to the first pew and studied the mural behind the altar. It was painted years before he came, the feast at Cana, a favorite among parishioners in those days. Martin knew that Christ had bristled at being expected to perform a miracle at Cana and had spoken harshly to His mother. As Martin sat there people walked around outside the church looking closely at each window. One woman entered behind him. He heard her say, "What a pretty church," and he knew she would not venture further inside. He took his Missal out of his pocket and began reading the Gradual from the proper of St. Agatha. He had chosen the passage essentially at random, but when he read it he was shocked:

> *"God will help her with his favorable countenance; God is with her;*
> *She shall not be disturbed. The stream of the river maketh the city*
> *of God joyful; the Most High hath sanctified his own tabernacle."*

Was what Martin had seen Christ's "favorable countenance"? Was He somehow sanctifying his tabernacle here at St. Agatha's? Impossible. Yet the missal lay plainly before him. Had Martin done wrong in taking out the window?

On Saturday more people came to look at the window. Ben Nagoda pulled his pickup truck on the grass near the vestry and stood for a while in its bed explaining what he had seen to the parishioners, locals from Mountain View and Hilo, and tourists down from Volcano. "I seen it plain as day," he told them at one point. "It was the face of Christ Almighty, the Lord Himself."

"Was it weeping?" a woman's voice called out.

"I think it was weeping," Ben said. He was a husky man, with a profound neck and a deep brow. "I think he was weeping for

91

Hawaiians throughout the islands. He was weeping for us."

"Someone said He tried to talk."

"I saw His lips move," Ben said. Martin cringed in the vestry. "I think He was trying to say a prayer."

Mrs. Manaloto offered to bring Martin his lunch, but he had no appetite. She looked both fearful and disappointed. "I saw His face," she said.

"It was the weather, the lightning did something to the glass. You saw what you wanted to see."

"Was there lightning? I don't remember lightning."

"You were probably in the kitchen."

"But you saw it too. That's why you put the pillowcase there."

"Yes. I can't explain it. Maybe we were seeing things."

She looked at him suspiciously and then looked at the window. "There's nothing there now" she said.

"The koa trees."

"But in the glass. There is nothing to see."

"No."

He feared that this madness would disturb Mass on Sunday. But luckily it did not. His usual altar boys, Uleki Holokahiki and Palani Kalihana, served for him. They arrived early and managed to sneak looks both outside and inside the vestry. They prepared everything with unusual industry and this Sunday they neither dropped the monstrance nor spilled the wine. They had asked him about the vision of the Volcanic Jesus, which is what it had become by the ten o'clock news on Saturday, and Martin desperately held back his anger and frustration. Uleki's excitement could hardly be contained. "It was a miracle they say. What makes it a miracle?"

"Nothing was a miracle. People thought it was an image of Our Lord," he told him, looking also at Palani to be sure he got the benefit of his wisdom. "You should know better. Go look for yourself."

They came back with a hangdog look. For a moment he regretted disappointing them.

He managed his way through Mass and offered Communion to the handful of regular members. He knew they all wanted him to talk about the Vision, as they called it, and while he wanted to talk about the question of God's creation of evil, he found he was able to do neither.

At the great table afterward, while Mrs. Manalato served tea and coffee, he finally found himself face to face with Auntie Violet. She held herself up with the aid of two canes. Her girth seemed enlarged from only a week earlier. She complained to him in a strange and commanding voice. "What kind of God would create hell up there in the caldera, where you can smell the devils about their work, and then present His face here in your vestry?"

She was at it again. "I am not sure that was Our Lord that people saw."

"It was God," Alema Kalihana said. "Mary told me she had seen God's face and that He smiled at her. Howard saw Him, too. He told me plainly. I was working in Hilo or I would have seen it too."

"Why has the image gone?" a voice asked.

"Because God torments His people," Auntie Violet said without looking back to see who had spoken. "This God has created evil and now cannot control evil."

"Auntie Violet," someone exclaimed in disbelief.

"I will speak about the creation of evil," Martin said. "But not now. And we must not risk blasphemy because we are under stress at the moment."

"You can smell His works up the road," Auntie Violet said. "Now He torments us with His image."

"You didn't see it," Howard Kalihana said. "If you'd seen it you wouldn't talk this way. It was, like, I don't know what. But it filled me up with a feeling. You shoulda seen little Mary the way she

93

looked. She was blessed by that vision. I damn well say she was blessed and maybe if you were there you'd a been blessed too. You coulda thrown away those crutches."

"They're canes," Ben Nagoda said softly. "Canes."

"Canes, then. You coulda thrown away those canes."

"What did you throw away?" Auntie Violet asked him. "What parts of your crippled heart did you throw away?"

Howard was flustered. "I threw away my wantin' to drink," he said finally. "I saw Him there and I said to myself He wants me to give up the booze. Alema can tell you."

Alema shook her head. "It's true. He's not touched a drop since Thursday, thank God."

Auntie Violet looked at him skeptically. "He'll be back at it by next Sunday."

"I don't think so," Ben Nagoda said. "I got the same message. 'Turn your life around,' it said to me. I know I gotta straighten things out with the Lord. I know that. I seen him watchin' me and the look on His face was something, you bet. I never seen nothin' like it. And when I said a prayer inside my head, the tears on His face showed up and I knew He heard me. I knew it and I went up to Honomu and told Mina I'm a new man. I told her she could come back and I'd spend my life makin' that woman happy. I don't mind tellin' you all. You know me. You all know me–or at least most of you know me." He nodded in recognition of the tourists in St. Agatha's. He tried to say something else, but then pressed his hands to his face. Martin saw that he was crying. People watched him uneasily.

Howard Kalihana approached Ben about to put his arm around him, but held back and only touched his shoulder. "It's okay," he said. "I felt it too."

Margaret Mahanamoa stepped forward and spilled some of her coffee on the floor as she reached for Ben Nagoda. "What was it?" she asked. "I wasn't there. I was out with Lanny at Hilo Hattie's.

94

What did you see?"

"The devil's work," Auntie Violet said coarsely. She stamped her canes loudly. "You'll see next week these two."

"It was Our Lord," Ben Nagoda said, touching Margaret's wrist. "I saw Him plain as day in the vestry window. And now He's gone."

"It was to tell us to straighten our lives."

"But why did He leave?" Margaret asked. "Why didn't He stay so I could see Him too?" She directed these last words to Martin.

"I don't know," he said. If Ben Nagoda and Howard Kalihana were truly as moved as they appeared, then maybe he was wrong in taking out the window. He thought of it now resting in his upstairs closet, wrapped in two large bath towels behind his moth proof garment bags. "It's possible," he said slowly, fearfully, "possible that there was some meaning to it."

"Yes," said Howard.

"He was trying to speak to me," Ben Nagoda said. "I felt it in my heart. You know how you feel things and then you get cold all over. That's what happened. I felt Him in my life."

Martin wondered how Ben could keep this up if he had not truly felt something that had changed him. Nothing Martin said or did for fifteen years changed Ben Nagoda from a brawling drunk to what he seemed to be today: a new man. Redemption was within the grasp of every Christian, even Ben Nagoda.

"You have been enriched," Martin said, adopting his pastoral tone. "Beyond measure, and beyond our capacity to understand. It is the way the Lord works in our daily lives."

"Is the experience only for them?" Margaret asked. "Am I left out?" She seemed pained and emotionally withered at the thought.

"I think," Martin said, "that if the Lord showed His countenance to St. Agatha's, that you are St. Agatha's. You are His church."

"What was it He showed to Moses?" Auntie Violet asked with a mock tremor to her voice.

Adeline Toshi, who taught Bible class to the children once a month spoke up. "The hind parts of God, of course."

Auntie Violet shook with laughter. "Crazies. God mooned Moses. He mooned Moses. And look what happened to Moses and to everybody afterward. What makes you think it be different here and now? What makes you think so?"

"St. Agatha was an early martyr," Martin said. "She looked on God full face, and saw the beatific light that the angels see and she was filled with that light just as some of you feel you have been filled. It is the light of God that illuminates the dark cottage of the soul in its tribulation here on earth. With that light within us all good things are possible, all manner of divine instruction can be ours and our lives can accept the richness of blessings reserved only for the righteous. We must try to be among the righteous." He became aware that he was delivering an extempore sermon and that people stood with their breakfast cakes halfway to their mouths or with their coffee suspended in air. He worried that these words, intending to put people at peace, were the product of his own hypocrisy and therefore perhaps of the devil's work. Auntie Violet's crazy talk may have had some validity if only to tell him that he must decide how to be truthful to an experience so improbable and so unlikely that he should, rightly, have nothing to do with it. Yet that was impossible. He thought that the image in the window was nothing more than a false witness to the insecurities and fear of people unable to conceive of their own blessedness without some manifestation in the material world to which they paid so much attention.

At least that was how he began his thinking, and that thinking guided him in removing the window. He wanted no circuses at St. Agatha's. Monsignor Lewis in leeward Oahu would call him in on the carpet if Martin let this become the kind of thing he saw on the news from the mainland. And he wanted as little to do with Monsignor Lewis as possible. He was a free man at St. Agatha's. No one could envy him his mission on the slopes of the volcano. Yet, the reaction of these people to the image their imagination had enlarged so grossly was one of pious enlightenment.

"Is it true you removed the window Friday night, Father?" Martin looked to see where the voice had come from. Slowly, through the group behind the great table, Jeff Pollitt and Jimmy Beniwa, the reporters, made themselves visible to him. "I thought I touched some wet paint when I saw the window."

"It's not the same kind of glass as the other windows," Jimmy Beniwa said. He looked around at the people in the meeting room. "He took the window out so you wouldn't see what these folks here saw, the image of Christ. He did it." He turned to look at Martin, who could not speak unless he spoke truthfully.

"Did you do that, Father?" Margaret asked him. Martin looked past her to see Mrs. Manaloto moving from the kitchen with another tray of nicely sliced fruit cakes. He saw a spot of fright on her face.

"You don't have to ask him," Jeff Pollitt said. "We checked. Yesterday I got a bright idea and went down to Kaufmann's and asked around about who was buying window glass and guess what? Father Martin here bought a pane of glass just the same size as the vestry window and he also bought some putty and some paint." He paused dramatically.

Ben Nagoda turned toward Martin. "Is that true, Father?"

Martin felt weak in the knees. This was too much. He held his hand to his chest and looked around for a chair. Mrs. Manaloto reacted as if he were having another attack and gave the tray to the nearest woman and pushed forward a folding chair in time to help Martin slump into it. Martin suddenly felt much older than his years. Auntie Violet stamped her canes as if she were demanding an

97

explanation.

"Where is it?" Howard asked. "Where did you put it?"

"How could you do that, Father Martin?" Margaret Mahanamoa asked him. "How could you deny us the vision?"

"That's probably why He was crying," Ben Nagoda said suddenly.

"He wasn't crying at all," Martin said, remembering how Ben Nagoda described His tears earlier. "We are the only ones who will be crying."

"Did you break the window, Father?" Howard asked.

"No. I didn't break anything."

"Where is it?" Jeff Pollitt asked.

Martin saw the looks on the faces of his small community and wondered how he would make them understand. "I did this out of love for St. Agatha's," he said.

"Funny way of showing love." Auntie Violet said flatly. "You take a sign like that and bury it so nobody else can see it."

Martin was again aware of Auntie Violet's inconsistencies and failed once more to understand her purposes. "Don't you see what is already happening here? Don't any of you see what you risk?"

Margaret Mahanamoa said, "All I want is to be able to see what Howard and Little Mary saw."

At this, Little Mary Kalihana came from the playroom at the back of the meeting room and stood by Martin. As he slumped in the folding chair, she was about as tall as he. Her eyes were a subtle hazlenut color with dark resonant pupils. Her lips were full and her cheeks flushed. She looked at Martin, then at her mother. "Where did God go?" Mary Kalihana asked. "I went to see Him and He is gone. Where did He go?" Martin could not tell whether Mary was distressed or simply disappointed. She was an unusual child, especially the way she had reacted to the window on Thursday night. He took her cool, moist hand and thought how simple life would be if little children could really lead him into enlightenment.

"God has not gone," Martin said. "God is where you are, wherever you are."

"He was in the window and now He is gone."

"Where is the window?" Jeff Pollitt repeated.

"It was to keep our community safe and sane. That was why I removed the window. This is not a vision of God, it is a simple phenomenon of chemistry or minerals or electricity. I don't know what, but I have seen churches torn apart by things like this. Or at least, I have heard of churches that have become zoos trying to please TV and newspapers and all manner of religious fakers. Don't you see . . . can't you see why we need to keep this all to ourselves?"

"It's news, father," Jimmy Beniwa said. The pulsing flashes from his Nikon stunned Martin for an instant. His eyes did not respond quickly and the red after glow on his retina made everything seem indefinite.

"But it is not Good News," he said, thinking of the Word.

"Of course it's good news. That's why we mean to report it. That's why the window has got to be replaced. You know where it is, and you'll have to have it put back right away."

"I don't have to do anything," Martin said. "I don't want us to be caught up in the kind of nonsense that you are already pressing on us."

Auntie Violet stamped forward. "When God created evil, could he have had this kind of evil in mind?"

"What does she mean?" Jimmy asked.

"She's got a thing about evil," Howard said. "She'll be okay."

"God created evil, and He created it for us. Not for Him. He is above it. It's like He's in a cruise ship while we struggle in the ocean of evil that He has created. He is above it. We are of it and in it, and God laughs at us from time to time. That face you saw was not crying. It was laughing. And it was laughing at you."

Some of the curious who had come to Mass recoiled. They probably never heard anyone speak like this in a church, especially in front of their pastor. Yet, he encouraged it and now felt he could do without it. Auntie Violet might be a bit unwound, yet, she seemed aware of the significance of her position and her constant declamations and impossible questions. He could not stifle her. He could not turn her away. St. Agatha was martyred for less, yet she must not be ignored.

"Father, you must restore the window," Howard told him. "Margaret should see it, and so should others. It's selfish to keep this only for ourselves."

Adeline Toshi, who had been to the University and who had helped in the Sunday School for several years, spoke up. "The Bible says God reveals Himself among us in many ways. I have not seen the window, but from what Ben Nagoda and others say, it has a great power to set lives straight and to inspire the faithful. Father Martin, is there nothing we can do? Is there no way to restore the window with His image?"

"It will bring destruction on us," Martin said, trying not to sound like a prophet, but not entirely sure he was not a prophet.

On Monday morning, Howard Kalihana and Ben Nagoda came to the vestry and removed the new window, which they said had been clumsily installed. "It woulda fell out by itself," Ben said when he put the glass down by the sitting chair. "Lookit this," he said, holding a warped strip of putty. Obviously the work of an amateur.

They had finally persuaded Martin to tell them where he put the window and while Martin knelt on the altar before the pyx saying his prayers, hoping against hope that his world would not dissolve in religious hysteria, they re-installed it properly.

"It's pretty old glass," Howard said as he held it in the frame.

"And all you can see are ripples when you look at it on an angle. Look for yourself."

Ben closed one eye and held the frame at a stark angle. "Yeah. But head on. Lookit. It's Him. It's Our Lord."

"Careful. Be careful." Howard grew suddenly fearful.

Mrs. Manaloto came into the vestry. "Is it still there?"

"Check it out."

"He looks sad."

"I don't know," Howard said. "Maybe. Are there tears?"

"It feels cold, not wet," Ben said, touching the glass.

"Don't touch it," Mrs. Manaloto said. "That wouldn't be right."

Margaret Mahanamoa came in with her son Lanny. The two of them looked at the window and Margaret pulled Lanny to the floor and both knelt with their hands together in front of their face. "I feel it," she said. "I feel it, too." She began weeping. Lanny looked up at her, then back to the window, which Ben Nagoda held, now in its frame on Martin's desk.

"I'm gonna have to putty it up now. You can see it from outside when I get it put back, but I gotta work on it now."

The TV cameras arrived by nine a.m. Martin heard the various announcers' rundown on the window. Japanese television, mainland television, and the local stations all interviewed Ben Nagoda and Howard Kalihana, who told them how their witness of the Image of Christ had altered their lives and how they felt the holy spirit within them. They both swore they saw the image in the window weep and try to speak to them. Ben Nagoda went so far as to tell the announcers that he thought the image was mouthing the words, "God bless Hawaii." Jeff Pollitt got that message out on the wires instantly and Martin knew that headlines around the world would trumpet St. Agatha's on the slopes of Kilauea, tiny St. Agatha's, as a place so holy that God made Himself manifest to the faithful. And the unfaithful, as well.

When he took lunch in the kitchen with Mrs. Manaloto, the lawn by the vestry was filled with people staring up at the window and in some cases crying out ecstatically. Martin had some sherry in his lentil soup and tried to read his breviary while eating his garden salad. "I don't know what to do," he said.

"You needn't do anything," she said. "It's out of your hands."

"Yes. Yes, it was out of my hands from the very first."

"You couldn't have known."

"Known what?"

"How powerful it was, how people would be changed, what it all meant."

"I still don't know what it all means."

Mrs. Manaloto looked at him. "It sounds," she said, "as if you don't believe."

"As if I don't believe? You mean as if I'm a non-believer?"

"No, no. But as if you don't believe this is a manifestation."

"Of God? A manifestation of God? No. I don't believe that. I told you from the very first. People see what they need to see."

"Then apparently our community must need to see this," she said, and walked into the pantry and opened and closed several drawers noisily.

Monsignor Lewis took action almost immediately. Father Steven Aguilera came over from the Cathedral of Our Lady of Peace in Honolulu and presented a letter from the Bishop. Father Martin Lahiri, "having celebrated your eighty-fifth birthday," was being asked to retire graciously while Father Aguilera accepted the parish and grounds of St. Agatha. "I can't believe this," Martin said looking at the letter. "Why did His Reverence do this? What did I do to bring this down on me? St. Agatha's is my home, has been my home for years. It's where I hoped to end my days. It's where I hoped to be buried, there in the church cemetery." He gestured vaguely outside.

"I'm not sure I can explain. It's probably just your age?" Father Aguilera said.

"Nonsense. Do you know? Did they tell you? What did they say? Certainly they said something or you would not be here today."

"I do not know how to respond, Father."

"Martin. Just Martin will do."

"Yes, Father."

"Please tell me what you know."

"Signs such as this appear only rarely, and in places where one would hardly expect. You know the words of the Mass for St. Agatha, for her name day. This is the showing forth of the countenance."

"You believe that?"

"Honolulu believes it. I myself have seen His countenance in the window. It is indisputable, whether one is in the vestry or outside the vestry, it is the face of Our Lord. How it came to be there is another mystery, no more or less mysterious than what is recorded in your mural behind the altar."

"So you think it is a miracle?"

"I didn't say that quite."

"You implied it quite. Do you think the image in the window is a miracle?"

Father Aguilera ran his fingers down his prominent nose. "Yes, I think it seems to be a miracle. Do you not think so?"

"Certainly not."

"You say certainly. How can you be so certain? Are you saying you do not believe in miracles?"

Martin grimaced. Mrs. Manaloto had brought them a pot of tea which she had placed in a cozy. He reached for it and poured himself another cup. "You know as well as I do, Father Aguilera, that all Catholics must believe in miracles."

"Yes."

"So the answer is yes, I believe in miracles. But this is no miracle. It is a strange phenomenon, something to do with minerals in the very old glass of that window, something to do with the storm we had and nothing more. It is a natural phenomenon."

"How do you explain the resemblance to the image on the Shroud of Turin?"

"I don't. Maybe it's all our imagination. I don't pretend to explain anything."

"You know Our Lord multiplied the loaves and the fishes at Cana."

"Yes, I do. But I also know he abjured his disciples from telling anyone."

"Then John should not have written it down?"

"Perhaps not."

"That could be considered heretical."

"Everything could be considered heretical. If you were to consider that remark heretical I would think you an utter fool. What I am talking is simple, practical, and obvious. People will be here for as long as we permit them to think we believe along with them in what is probably a convenient figment of imagination and not a manifestation. I would rather we put the window away."

"As you did."

"As I tried to do.

"I can't understand, Father, why you would have done that without consulting Monsignor Lewis. How could you have done that?"

"It was my parish and my responsibility. Belief in Our Lord does not–should not–depend on a picture in a window that people think looks like another picture on a cloth. Don't you see that?"

"But think of the reports we have had from your own parishioners, how this experience has changed them."

"Yes, exactly what I mean. They think they see something that now makes them reform their lives. I tried to help them all understand the meaning of faith. And I know I sometimes failed to make things clear. But this undoes it all. It undoes all my work."

"Father . . . ."

"They take this . . . this vision, as a tangible fact, tangible evidence. Just as Auntie Violet takes the caldera in Kilauea as tangible evidence of hell and what she calls God's evil. Tangible. Do you have any idea what that means, tangible? It means that I have let my flock slump into the very materiality that we are constantly battling against in this society. It is faith, Father Aguilera, and only faith that will save us. You know that and I know that. Faith."

Father Aguilera made a few concessions to Martin. He permitted him to stay in his room above the vestry until the end of the month. And he permitted Martin to deliver the sermon on St. Agatha's name day, but it was understood that afterward, Martin was to report to Monsignor Lewis to discuss the arrangements the Bishop had made for his retirement. While Martin tried to face up to his responsibilities, Father Aguilera spent time with parishioners, visiting their homes, meeting with them in the vestry or the meeting room. Father Aguilera talked with the Kalihanas, the Mahanimoas, the Nagodas, the Toshis, the Changs, and even Auntie Violet, when she appeared before him, of the power of miracles. He told them how miracles reinforce faith, how great events seem sometimes to be presaged by visions of Our Lady. The parishioners knew about the manifestation at Lourdes and the mysterious sealed prophecy. Father Aguilera calmed everyone when Auntie Violet suggested that this sighting might be followed by an eruption of the recently active volcano. Was this a warning for them to leave, to flee? Father Aguilera had no idea, but he did what he could to calm everyone, even those who usually paid no attention to the rantings of Auntie

Violet. Later, he told Martin, he called the University Observatory on Mauna Kea and asked them directly what the chances of a major eruption might be. The response was more detailed and specific than he could possibly deal with, but as he understood it, the chances were very slim. He could honestly tell people that they need not fear a terrible event. Rather, he suggested, they might consider looking forward to a splendid event, although he was not specific. Martin overheard some of these discussions while he sat in the vestry or while he knelt in the first pew saying his prayers.

During the first evening after Father Aguilera arrived, people flocked to the lawn to see what the television stations had dubbed "The Volcanic Jesus." The term seemed thoroughly inappropriate to him, but it stuck. People came from all parts of the island to see the Volcanic Jesus, hoping it would begin to cry, or perhaps to move its lips and speak to them. At night, people stood with lighted candles. They chanted prayers at different times through their vigil. Father Aguilera kept a small lamp on in the Vestry so that the Image would be visible at all hours.

In a matter of days, people set up tables next to their vans with T-shirts in many colors, all with a replication of the image in the window. Martin heard shouting one day between competing merchants who accused each other of having "ripped them off" by plagiarizing their image. A lawyer from Honolulu came to St. Agatha's and told Father Aguilera and Martin very sternly that they had to copyright the image or risk losing it. Martin asked what he meant by "losing it," and the lawyer told him plainly: "Any one of the T-shirt salesmen out there can copyright the image in their own name and then demand a fee for its use. It's like an NBA logo. It's copyrighted. You can't just go and put it on your clothes and think you can get away with it." The lawyer offered to do the paperwork immediately, before anyone else "wised up."

Father Aguilera took his card, thanked him politely, called

Honolulu, and discovered that there had already been a move afoot in that direction. The diocesan legal team was on it.

Martin could not go anywhere without being quizzed on why he had taken the glass out of the window, and when he was asked he refused to comment. His picture appeared in the newspaper, usually with the perplexed look of an old man who had lost his way in a crowd. At night, when he tried to sleep, the mumbled prayers of candle-holding believers sometimes awoke him or prevented him from sleep altogether. Some of the sales people in the vans brought their entire families and stayed in St. Agatha's parking lot as if it were a campground. Father Aguilera installed five outdoor porta-potties as a means of keeping the church's inadequate plumbing from being overwhelmed. He finally had to make it plain that no one was to enter the vestry to see the window from the inside. However, people were welcome in the church proper, especially when they entered and prayed.

Martin knew his years were catching up to him. The stress, his anger, loss of sleep, and the bewildering activity upsetting the routine he had so carefully established–all this served to deprive him of his sense of balance. All the madness he predicted descended on St. Agatha's, and he was completely powerless to stop it, control it, or understand it. Mrs. Manaloto now served both Father Aguilera and him, and she often looked as if she were deeply worried about him. He had always expected that age would soften the journey to the grave, by slowly numbing his awareness of the world around him. But now he had the feeling that age rendered him incapable, while leaving him all the more aware of his own decline.

The Saturday before his final Mass, Auntie Violet came to him. "You been dodging me, Father," she said. "You tell me what this all comes down to. You tell me why you did what you did."

"You mean about the window."

"The Volcanic Jesus. How did you make that window do

that?"

Martin almost laughed. "I didn't make the window do anything."

"People say you took that window and soaked it in a special chemical so it would show up a picture. They say it's like photography. You take it and soak it and there's the picture."

"Oh Lord," he said. He had to sit down behind his desk and signaled Auntie Violet to do the same, but she stood there on her two canes, stamping each one softly as she kept her balance. "I don't know who told you that, but it's nonsense."

"You said yourself it was a chemical change."

"Could be, I said. Could be a chemical change. Something to do with metals in the old glass. I don't know anymore than you do."

"If you did that, then you are part of the evil. To fool all those people is evil."

"Yes, you are right. It is evil. I said that, too. Right from the beginning. We do not need people out there selling T-shirts, rosaries, and abalone crucifixes. When He was alive, He would have cast them from his temple."

"Which you should do."

"It is no longer mine. You'll have to speak to Father Aguilera."

"He doesn't talk to me."

"How do you mean?"

"They think I am crazy."

"And you're not?"

"No more than you."

Father Aguilera said Mass, but left time for Martin to deliver the sermon, as he promised. Storm clouds gathered the evening before and a heavy, although customarily brief, rain had swept through, dampening the spirits of the evening's candle holders.

Despite their absence, Martin found himself growing more confused. He was not quite sure how to proceed and he began by quoting from his missal for St. Agatha's, "I invoke him, the living God, who vouchsafed to heal all my wounds and to restore my breast to my body." But as he said the words, he knew that his wounds would not heal any more than that St. Agatha's church would return to its anonymous peacefulness. He saw that these people were, along with him, all lost. They had given themselves over to their craving for reassurance, for certainty, for proof of the love of God.

"My wounds grow daily," he said. The pews were not full, but the light after the storm passed through grew especially radiant and the air refreshed. He breathed deeply. "Auntie Violet has said repeatedly that it is difficult to love a God who would create evil and submit us all to its forces. And evil is forceful, as you all know. Now, there are some who say evil was not created by God, but by Satan, and we all know that Satan was created by God. But of course he was created as Lucifer, the light bearer. Satan created himself as Satan, according to some, but we know, too, that only God is the creator. Satan has created nothing. Satan is the adversary, the destroyer. Knowing that, we come back to the question of evil. Was it created by God? Let me read to you from Isaiah, 'I am the Lord, and there is none else, there is no God besides me: I girded thee, though thou hast not known me; that they may know from the rising of the sun, and from the west, that there is none besides me. I am the Lord, and there is none else. I form the light, and create darkness: I make peace, and create evil: I the Lord do all these things.'

"So Auntie Violet told the truth when she said God created evil. And all the more truthful was she when she said it was created for us and not for God. Why would God create evil for Himself? He created it for us, to test us, to permit us to conduct ourselves through life not as people for whom all is given as if on a golden platter. But as people who can learn to achieve innocence and be, as He said, like

109

little children."

He sensed anxiety in the front pews and wondered if he were wandering. His thoughts were growing unclear and his head throbbed. He looked to see if Father Aguilera were distressed, but he sat across the way with his eyes closed.

"Some say, along with St. Augustine, that evil is nothing, the absence of good. But if so, how could God have created it? We are told that God created light, but did He not also create the darkness?" More stirring in the pews. He paused. "The image of God in the window is not evil. Do not make that mistake. I removed it not because it was evil, but because I thought it would lead us away from the light, and toward the darkness. Away from God's good and possibly toward God's evil. Perhaps I was wrong in removing it. I admit to being wrong many times in my life. Had I left it there, perhaps the television people would have treated this all differently. I don't know. I see the T-shirts and I wonder how many forms evil can take, and whether somehow the commercialization of this phenomenon is something we should fear. Such things happened in Christ's lifetime. We know that. He was unsympathetic toward it, and so am I."

Father Aguilera opened his eyes.

"Let me say," Martin began, "that I am sorry. I am sorry to leave you with all this . . . this nonsense distorting the mission of St. Agatha's. Our church now appears on a map that I saw only a few days ago describing the Miracle of St. Agatha's, and we will soon have pilgrims from all over the world coming to see our vestry window. I won't be here."

As he said these last words he felt a stabbing pain and lowered himself to one knee. He had no idea what was happening to him, but as he knelt he raised a hand in benediction and the entire church moved forward to its knees as if on his signal. But when he slowly fell to the floor, they rose suddenly and watched Father

Aguilera rush over to try to pick him up.

Auntie Violet was by no means satisfied with Martin's final sermon. Even at his funeral, she ranted about his having fallen into the grip of evil. Martin got his wish and was buried in the sanctified burial ground beside the church, in full view of the window which was now framed, protected by unbreakable glass, and sheltered with a housing that included indirect lighting so that the image of Our Lord could be seen twenty-four hours a day. No one who heard Auntie Violet could make sense of her complaints, and certainly no one thought, as she did, that Martin was in the arms of the devil, despite his resistance to the development of St. Agatha's into a pilgrimage destination. The congregation tolerated her out of reverence to Father Martin, but most people thought she was as crazy as she seemed, especially when she threatened to follow him into the realm of Dis if need be in order to satisfy her need to understand God's evil.

Auntie Violet implied that Martin's death was somehow connected with his views on the nature and origin of evil. All of what he said, she told people, did nothing more than confirm her own strange and uncertain views. And she, too, grew angry at the constant swarm of pilgrims and the merchants who made it all but impossible for her to come to St. Agatha's in peace and quiet. And she despised Father Aguilera, who paid no attention to her at all and refused to respond to her constant questions, such as what would happen if an island rat were to eat the consecrated host. Would the rat enter the precincts of heaven? She was filled with questions that no one could address for her.

So it was that she decided to take her questions on the nature of evil and pose them in the precincts, not of heaven, but of hell. In the lee of a frightening storm, she had Arthur Chang's taxicab service deliver her to the rim of Kilauea crater at the inn at Volcano House as if she were planning a weekend. But when the cab turned around, she began the painful journey upward and away from the inn. When she was a young girl her grandfather Able Takamiya took the entire family for a weekend's stay at the inn and showed her first hand the celebrated caldera at Kilauea. She had recoiled at the sulphurous odors that rose day and night from the cooling black lava and the curling steam vents, but she was also transfixed by the thought that this was where the devil secreted himself when not abroad in the world.

Auntie Violet placed her canes before her and moved forward to reach the asphalted Devastation Trail, which she recalled from childhood. The scrubby ohia trees surprised her because they were not there when she was a child. Much had changed. As she made her way along the trail toward the lava tubes the storm began to make the trees sway and she felt the first drops of rain. Out on the caldera before her she saw the steam vents giving way in all directions. At the end of the asphalted trail, she reached her canes forward and saw that they held on the black crusty lava slope. She moved forward calling, "You devils have him. I know you have him and I want him back. He never answered my questions. You have him. I want him back. Do you hear me?" The rain, now heavy, turned to steam as it touched the caldera surface near Auntie Violet, and the storm smothered her voice, rising now in anger, with the tumult of lightning and the rolling of thunder.

Never Turn Your Back on the Sea

They had been warned, true, but Polly Werner and Kate Galway, vacationing at The Cabins in Haena for their second winter, thought they knew how the sea worked, just as they knew how the young Hawaiian men sat with mellow eyes trolling the beaches for affection. That was part of their pleasure, too. Both divorced, they took their daughters on their vacations and helped each other develop special friendships. This year, Polly's friend was a yoga teacher from Romania, living simply in the fashion of a holy man, on the beach, in the state park, and even for a time in her cabin. Rusk picked up his English on his way from Bombay to Singapore and then to Hawaii. It was rudimentary, but serviceable. And as it happened, Polly enjoyed his thoughts, leavened as they were with a series of encounters with gurus, mystics, and yoga-stretching girlfriends. His few words implied that he was on a spiritual quest.

Her quest was a bit different. Rusk professed love, but also told her he needed to know that when the rains came he would not have to sit huddled under his North Slope hand-me-down with the ground turning to mud under his sleeping bag. She assured him that during this January he need fear no monsoon, and she took him to her bed with the full knowledge that when she left she would probably never see him again.

Polly and Kate, both Toronto girls, lived side by side in a two-family cottage in the Beaches near the turn-around of the tram track. Polly worked in data processing. Kate was a consultant for York TV. Rusk showed up one day at The Cabins in Haena after bicycling over the dozen or so one-lane bridges that took him to the edge of the Na

Pali cliffs looking out at the wild ocean. Rusk could have charmed either woman, but after he gave her what he called a healing massage, Polly appropriated him for herself with Kate's blessing.

Polly's Adelle was a whiny child, quick to blame her mother for any disappointment. She said she liked Rusk, but she knew that he preferred Kate's daughter, Madeleine, 13, who was older by four years and listened to him when he told stories about wonder workers in remote villages on the Andaman Islands and other outlandish places. Every so often, when Madeleine snubbed her, Adelle sulked in her room. But whenever they were indoors, Madeleine just read her books while Adelle played with Beachfront Barbie and Ken or made up silly games. Madeleine said she thought Rusk was a cool dude. She knew he smoked the local marijuana, and while she was wary of all kinds of dope, Rusk's laid-back Eastern style made him an exotic. Her father, now living in Detroit, called such people degenerates, and Madeleine was curious about degenerates.

The wave came without warning, just as locals told them it might.

Adelle was in her room sulking, Madeleine was halfway through *The Lord of the Rings*, and Polly, after "getting her legs wet" in the foamy surf, walked up the sand to their beach towels. Rusk had cycled into Hanalei to get some food at the Big Save with Polly's credit card–he sometimes signed her name "Mickey Mouse," just for fun. Polly was already dry when she turned and began to signal Kate. Kate, in up to her knees, waved back to her and got the message: Polly was ready to leave. It was time to roll up the reed mats and put everything into the Coleman Chest and get the children ready for lunch when Rusk returned.

Polly heard a crash on the sand behind her, thought she heard a call from Kate, then looked up at three young Hawaiian men running down to the sea yelling and calling.

Kate had vanished.

The wave came up behind her and pulled her out to sea in a matter of seconds. Polly turned and searched the white caps on the edge of the sand, then looked further out at the level ocean and beyond to the deep emerald swells ready to rise and break on the shore. Kate was gone. Not an arm, not a leg, not a sign of her. Polly screamed as if somehow she could call her back. The three men stopped short of plunging into the water.

"She's gone," the tallest man said. "It pulled her right out and down under the wave."

"Never turn your back on the sea," the short dark young Hawaiian man said. "We tell them all the time, specially now, this month. You never turn your back on the sea. Swallow you right up, the sea."

"I'll get the phone" the third man said. He ran back up the beach.

Polly stood there transfixed. "Do something," she said. "You have to do something," she said, running down to the surf. The young Hawaiian ran after her and pulled her back.

"You'll die, too," he said, half out of breath.

"She has to be there."

"She's gone."

"No. No." Polly fought against the young man and fell to her knees and began to scream. "It can't be." She could not control herself. She cried until she thought of Madeleine and tried to imagine how she would tell her. Polly struggled to calm herself.

"It's not your fault," the young man said.

"I know, I know. But what happened?"

"It's the wave," he said. "You never turn your back on the sea around here because the wave pulls you under so fast you can't fight it."

The other man who had used the phone came back. "Let's get the rigger."

They ran through the trees across the sand to the apartments down the beach and dragged out what looked like a ceremonial outrigger, and shoved it into the water, following with their paddles. They crested the first wave, then moved aslant the incoming waves and located themselves relative to where Kate had been pulled in. Polly was instructed to stand where she last saw Kate so they could gauge their search. He told her if Kate were still alive that would be the best way they could find her. Polly tried to be calm. She scanned the waters, hoping for a sign of Kate. If she were alive, she would see her. She was sure. Unless the current pulled her down toward the cliffs and out of sight. That was possible. But the men in the outrigger moved back and forth in front of her, going out as far as they dared. They went over the area out from the beach, back and forth for more than twenty minutes. They came back without seeing anything or anyone.

"This can't happen," she said. She was frantic with fear. "This can't happen," she said again, looking at the three young men. "My God." She couldn't think straight. What was she to do? How could Kate just disappear like that?

The emergency crew pulled up in a small white van near Polly. The nurses, a man and a woman, listened as a young blonde policeman questioned the men from the outrigger. "It's what happened to Sisero last week," the shortest Hawaiian man said. The policeman nodded. They all walked down to the last place they had seen Kate. Polly went with them, trying to hear what they said.

"Bad today." The policeman scanned the water with binoculars. "I don't see anything."

"She gone. We went out with the 'rigger and didn't see nothing," the shortest Hawaiian said. Polly saw how powerful his upper body was when he gestured to the policeman. "That woman gone."

"You next of kin?"

Polly tried to gather her thoughts. She knew Kate had to be out there. How could these people be so calm? "We're neighbors in Toronto. Can't you do something?"

"Ah," the policeman said, "Toronto."

"Can't you find her?"

"I called in our 'copter on the way out here," he said. "Look, you gotta realize we see this happen every so often. Was she a good swimmer?"

"Yes," and as she said the word, they heard the helicopter swirling in from the direction of the Na Pali coast, then saw it hover over the water, swooping slowly from side to side, covering the area the men in the outrigger had searched. But the helicopter took a wider swath and moved slowly from side to side, then after a long while it moved back out of sight toward the state park. Would the water have taken her that far?

With the sound of the helicopter, Madeleine and Adelle came running down from the cabin, anxious to know what happened. Polly didn't want to tell her that Kate was probably dead. She didn't know what to say.

"Where's mommy," Madeleine asked. Adelle looked baffled.

Polly, trembling, took Madeleine's hands. "There's been an accident. A wave . . . a big wave took her and she's lost."

"Lost?" Madeleine looked at the policeman. "My mommy's lost?" Her mouth hung open for an instant, and then she shrieked in such horror that Adelle broke out crying instantly. They both wailed painfully, both clinging to Polly who cried along with them. More and more people had begun to gather on the beach trying to figure out what happened. Polly and the children began crying with such visceral bodily wrenching that the bystanders gaped at them almost afraid to take another step forward. One of the nurses began to weep and put her arms around Polly and the children.

The policeman took a few steps away and placed his phone

to his ear. "They didn't see anything," he told the other nurse. "Not a sign."

"Whatta we do?" the muscular Hawaiian asked.

"Wait. It's all you can do."

By the time the nurses got Polly and the children back to their cabin, Adelle was hysterical, as if she had lost her own mother. Madeleine almost choked each time she took a breath between her screams for her mother. On the bed she shook so frighteningly that the nurse administered a strong sedative. She gave Adelle two pills and offered Polly a tranquilizer. At first, Madeleine's shakes grew more violent, timed to her hysterical crying, but in a few minutes she began to slow down and the shot took effect with her slipping into a mercifully unconscious state. Adelle clung to Polly and began hiccupping, but soon she slowed down.

In the middle of the hysterics, Rusk came wobbling up on the bicycle, plastic shopping bags hanging from the handlebars. He was bleary looking, clearly stoned, uneasy near the cop. He brought the groceries in and looked at the Hawaiian men sitting on the big wicker couch. He heard Polly and the children in the bedroom. "Hey, Keezu," he said. "What's up?" Keezu told him, explaining that he and his buddies had to stay to make the report. Rusk made some herb tea and brought it in to Polly. "Terrible," he said. "You saw it?" Polly nodded. She had just gotten Adelle to sleep in her arms and she couldn't speak. She shook her head sadly when Rusk offered her the tea. He went back to the living room and drank it himself. Keezu told him how they took the Seafarer's outrigger and scoured the area. Nothing there, he told Rusk.

"You remember Sisero?" he said.

Rusk nodded.

"Same thing. Last month. Can you figure? Sisero was major, man. He got took, just like that."

Rusk went back to check on Polly. She lay there weeping and

he touched her shoulder consolingly. Madeleine was on the other bed in an uncomfortable looking position, but she was breathing heavily–at peace at least for a while.

The policeman was in the living room taking a statement from Keezu and his friends. They explained everything again, correcting each other in certain details. When he finished he turned to Rusk. "You're not the father, right?"

"No. No. Friend is all."

"Where's the father? He here?"

Rusk shook his head.

"Where is he?"

Rusk shrugged. "Canada maybe?"

"Canada?"

"Divorced I heard."

"Right. How we gonna tell him? I gotta make contact with the husband."

The male nurse came through the front door. "We're taking the van back. You want me to have them send you a car?"

"I'll call later. I gotta stay until I get through to the father on this."

Rusk went into Kate's side of the cabin and found her purse. He decided not to open it, but to bring it back. Better that way. He handed it to the policeman. Keezu and his friends got up, finished with their part of this. "Later," Keezu said on the way out. Rusk nodded.

The policeman opened the purse and began to place various items on the kitchen table. "Kate Galway, right?"

Rusk nodded.

The policeman put Kate's wallet on the table, then her checkbook, her credit card case, a compact, two lipsticks, a comb, a small bag of instruments, then found a red leather address book. He found the name he wanted and moved to the phone. He got an answer machine and calculated the time in Detroit. If this was a work phone, then he would have left already. If it were a home phone, then he might be there or out to dinner. The policeman identified himself to the machine as Martin LaPaz and explained that there had been an accident involving Jeff's ex-wife and that he was needed in Hawaii as soon as possible.

Jeff called back in a little more than an hour. Polly was knocked out along with the children and when the phone rang Officer LaPaz picked it up and began describing the situation.

"My God," Jeff said. "Is Madeleine okay?"

Officer LaPaz explained that she was okay but that Kate had been pulled under by the wave. They were still searching, he told him, and they would keep looking through tomorrow.

"Is there any hope?"

"Frankly, not much. You never know, of course, but we don't hold out much hope here."

Officer LaPaz tried to explain what happened, reconstructing it as best he could from what Keezu and his buddies told him and what he could divine from Polly's tearful ramblings. Rusk nodded a couple of times in reinforcement when Officer LaPaz described the efforts of the helicopter crew and the boys out there with the outrigger. When he asked if he could speak with Madeleine, Officer LaPaz explained the situation and asked him to get the next plane out of Detroit and arrive in Lihue as quickly as he could. "I'll call as soon as I know when I'll be there."

The girls stayed asleep, but Polly rose in the evening around nine. She found Rusk on the floor of the living room in the lotus position before a yellow hibiscus floating in a bowl of water. He was meditating, he said, on life and death. When she told him she was hungry he took out two of the frozen veggie dinners he'd brought back and poured them both a tumbler of vodka on ice. He sliced a lemon and dropped a wedge in each glass. "We need live each day totally," he said. She'd heard that before.

"What I can't figure," she said, "is how fast it happened. I turned just for a moment to get the mats, and then she was gone. It was as if God had reached out of the heavens and pulled her out of the world."

"Could be fate."

They ate their meals silently. Polly listened for the girls, but there was no sound. Whatever the nurse gave them worked big time. Bless that nurse. Polly went in to check on them and saw that Madeleine had turned over and was in a better position. She put a light cover over her and saw that Adelle was okay.

"I sleep out here?" Rusk said, pointing to the wicker sofa.

"Tonight," she said. Rusk had his moments, but he was aware of her feelings.

Shortly after midnight Jeff called. "When I get to Honolulu, they'll put me on Aloha flight 109, so if I make it that'll get me to Lihue at 12:48 in the afternoon. How long to get to where you are?"

She told him it might take an hour and she explained that it would seem like he was going to the end of the world with all the one-lane bridges after Hanalei. She gave him precise directions while he wrote everything down.

"Madeleine is asleep right now. But give me your cell number. When she gets up I'll have her call you. She's all right. We had a nurse who gave her a sedative. She was really panicked. In fact, I'm still panicked." She told him that Kate's body had not turned up and that according to Officer LaPaz it might never turn up. She hated herself for using the term "Kate's body." She should have just said Kate hadn't turned up. She listened for a reaction from Jeff. "She was having such a good time," Polly said, realizing how lame that must sound.

She looked at Rusk when she put the phone down. "It was a

bad divorce. Lot of real hostility there. Kate gave up the house, but got custody of Madeleine for fifty weeks out of the year. Her father's a hard-liner."

Rusk looked mystified.

"I mean he's a tough-minded business man, very straight, very tough to deal with. He runs some kind of sports franchise. He doesn't like me and probably won't like you. Kate always had trouble with him. I haven't seen him in a long time, since he brought Madeleine back last summer."

Madeleine and Adelle were up with the first light. Polly was in a daze, but Rusk was wide awake and took Madeleine by the hand and sat down with her to talk about the beliefs of Hindu mystics who preached the doctrine of reincarnation. Madeleine listened, but when he was done, all she said was, "My mommy's dead, isn't she?"

"They think so," he said.

Madeleine held herself firmly. "When will Jeff be here?"

"You can call him," Polly said. "Jeff will be here this afternoon."

Madeleine took the phone to her side of the cabin and talked with her father for almost half an hour. When she began the conversation Adelle looked at Polly. "Are you going to die, too?"

"For God's sakes, no." Adelle's eyes suddenly began to fill. Polly held her close and regretted her tone. "Of course I won't die, sweetie. Please don't worry."

Madeleine returned with a resolute expression. "I'm going to live with Jeff and Julia," she said.

"You're moving?" Adelle said.

"I'm going to Detroit," Madeleine told her. "It's not that far."

"Someone new is moving next to us?" Adelle said to Polly.

"Please, sweetie. That's not important now." She looked at Madeleine. "You're being very brave. Are you all right?" Madeleine nodded.

Rusk took Madeleine into the kitchen. "I need help with breakfast," he told her. He held Madeleine's hand in both of his own and smiled at her.

"We could play dress-up," Adelle said.

"I'm going to help Rusk," she said. "You could do the toast," she said, aware of how awkward things were for Adelle.

Adelle jumped off the couch and got the bread out of the refrigerator. She was glad to have something to concentrate on. She was glad to have a chore.

Rusk showed Madeleine how to break an egg with one hand, then gave her the bowl of eggs and watched as she crushed several and got the albumen all over her fingers. It was sticky and she wiped her hands in the towel and then washed the towel. Her deep concentration made things seem almost normal. Rusk gave her a kiss on top of her head. "You did good, we get great eggs now." He helped her scoop out the tiny shards of eggshells.

Polly pointed to the half-gallon of Vodka. "Should we have a bloody Mary?"

"Sure. Morning support. You call it that?"

"Something like that."

"Can I do that?" Madeleine asked.

"Need expert," Rusk said.

"I do it for Jeff and Julia," she protested.

"Need taller expert." He made some drinks while Madeleine got two stalks of celery and trimmed them. She handed them proudly to Rusk, who bowed and placed his hands ceremoniously on her shoulders. "Thank you, celery expert."

They gathered at the kitchen table. Polly positioned Madeleine with her back to the ocean, which was magnificent and painterly this morning. Rusk sat on Madeleine's side of the table, and Adelle sat across from Madeleine. Before they ate, they all held hands and Rusk said, "Right action, right speech, right thought, right food."

"How are the eggs?" Madeleine asked, sounding like her mother.

"Expert!" Rusk said with a flourish.

"Expert," Adelle said.

Jeff called later that afternoon. He was in Lihue but there was a problem getting his car. He talked with Madeleine for fifteen minutes and Polly was taken with how grown up she seemed, as if she assumed her mother's role in life now that Kate was gone. Polly heard Madeleine mention her name as well as Rusk's–something she wished she hadn't done. She did not know how much Jeff knew about her and Kate's vacations, but he must have had an inkling.

Madeleine gave Polly the telephone and Jeff asked who Rusk was. "My friend," she said simply. "He's been good. He's been very good to Madeleine."

Jeff was a tall, black-haired, handsome man. His torso was thick, his shoulders huge, and his hands massive. His physical presence was that of a man who commanded extraordinary space. He had played Canadian football for several years in Calgary and seemed outsized in relation to most other men. He spoke with a commanding voice and examined people with sharp, dark eyes and an expression that seemed to mean he was about to say something, but held back. When he arrived, he moved toward the cabin and found Madeleine running to meet him on her way out. Jeff picked Madeleine up and swung her around, telling her it was going to be okay, that he was here now, and that everything was all right. When he put her down Madeleine was teary, but in control. "Mommy's gone," she said. "They think she's dead."

"Who says that?" he asked Polly.

"The police. They say this kind of thing happens here."

"Did you know about that when you rented the cabin?"

"They said it could be dangerous, so we were always careful. Especially the children."

"Never go in the water alone," Madeleine said. Adelle stood in the doorway twisting one leg around the other. She didn't know Jeff.

Rusk came out of the bathroom. He'd just brushed his teeth and combed his hair. "This is Rusk," Madeleine said, introducing him.

"So sorry," Rusk said. "Kate was nice."

Jeff nodded. "But what did they tell you when you got this place," he asked Polly.

"We were here last year," Polly said. "We never went into the water to swim. They showed us how to use boogie boards, but we hardly ever used them. We'd just watch the water and the sky and the trees . . . ." She began to feel herself getting too emotional. "God, we never thought . . . ."

Jeff looked at Rusk. "I don't swim," Rusk said, shrugging his shoulders.

Jeff stood up and took Madeleine outside to see where Kate had been and to talk with her about what they should do. Rusk looked over to Adelle. "You don't know Jeff?" Adelle shook her head. "Why don't you go out and meet him." She shook her head again. In a moment, she went back into her room and Polly heard her talking softly in the voices of Barbie and Ken.

"I thought he was going to take my head off," Polly said. "I know he blames me. It was my idea coming here on our vacation. He didn't want Kate to take Madeleine at all. I don't think he wanted Kate to go, either. It was a very bad divorce. In the papers. He never forgave her for getting custody of Madeleine and the way she tried to keep him away. He was a bit out of control in the early part of the proceedings. He's the kind of man who always gets his own way, and at one point I really thought he might hurt her. I did what I could to protect Kate, and he thinks I'm a bad influence."

"You are," Rusk said.

"Come on, we had a great time last year. Nothing happened, nothing went wrong. We all had more fun. I thought this was going to be even better. Now look. I still have the feeling Kate's going to walk in the door and ask what all the fuss was about."

"I don't think so."

Polly twisted the fringe of the sofa cushion and stretched her feet out on the table. "Nothing will ever be the same, now."

Jeff came back. "Madeleine and I need some dinner. Where should we go?"

"We can do something right here."

"It's quicker if we go out."

Jeff drove all of them back to Zelo's, an open-air beach house restaurant in Hanalei. He stared at the tropical decor and ordered a Beck's. Rusk and Polly had spaghetti with the children, and Jeff ordered the cajun chicken. Adelle finally found her voice and told Jeff quietly, "I really liked Kate."

He gave her a nod of recognition. "Thanks."

Jeff wanted to take Madeleine to another hotel for the night, but nothing was available, so he did what Polly asked him to do. She wanted him to stay with Madeleine in the cabin. There was enough privacy for both of them. Back at the cabin, Jeff took Polly outside alone.

"What is this guy, a gypsy?"

"He's Romanian. He teaches Yoga across from the restaurant."

"Madeleine says he smokes dope."

"Everybody out here smokes dope."

"Not everybody. What does Madeleine see in him?"

"He's very spiritual. He's great with her. When Kate died he tried to help her understand . . . ."

"We don't know yet that she's dead."

"But when she was taken it was Rusk who helped her most. I was a basket case."

"I don't want him near her."

"You'll have to tell her yourself. She's not going to like hearing that."

"I wish I had brought Julia. She'd know what to do," he said. They had wandered away from the cabin and the insistent sound of the waves made them both study the darkness. "What's this Rusk fellow to you?"

"Friend."

"You sleep with him?"

"Jesus!"

"Did he sleep with Kate?"

"I'm not going to answer that either. But he's my friend, not Kate's, although Kate liked him and thought he was good for Madeleine, a good male influence."

"Well, she's got me as her male influence now," he said and walked back to the cabin.

Despite what they said about the sea, Kate's body washed up on the Na Pali coast, battered, almost unrecognizable, early the next evening. Although Jeff still had trouble with jet lag, he stayed alert so that he could keep Madeleine away from Rusk. But when Officer LaPaz called around ten p.m. with the news, Jeff had to go by himself to identify the body. Rusk stayed with Polly and the children and talked with Madeleine about her feelings.

"What's Detroit like?" she asked.

Rusk shrugged his shoulders. "Cars, I think."

"It's nice," Polly said.

"Can we come and visit?" Adelle asked.

"Julia says I can have my room there. My summer room."

"And you'll have your father," Rusk said. "Is good for you to have your father."

Jeff returned a shattered man. "I don't know what to say," he told Polly. They sat on the screened veranda. "I just saw her six months ago when I brought Madeleine back from her visit. She seemed adjusted pretty well to the divorce and everything. She was getting her life together. You know, I talked with her for fifteen minutes or so when I dropped Madeleine off, and I thought to myself, this whole thing has been for the best. Julia was so terrific with Madeleine. I mean, they went out shopping together and they had lunch in Lord and Taylor and I thought, it's like having two mothers. And in a way, Kate never looked better. She was even civil to me for a change. Then I went down to the hospital here, still thinking there had to be a big mistake. It couldn't be Kate. It just couldn't be, and when they took the sheet back I really wasn't sure it was Kate. I mean, I looked at this body and I asked myself, is this the woman I used to be married to? Could this be the body of a woman I once loved? It was terrible looking. Almost not even human looking." He put his face in his hands. "It was this thing I was looking at, something out of the ocean, like it was prehistoric. Blue and battered because the rocks around the coast or something are so terrible they just sliver and cut the flesh of anyone out there, and she was long dead when the waves battered her on the rocks."

Now he lost control of himself and Polly moved to him and put her hand on his shoulder. Rusk had been standing with the closed door behind him, watching Jeff, almost holding his breath. Jeff began to sob, his chest heaving suddenly as he gasped for breath. Rusk stepped briskly forward and moved next to him on the divan. "Come here," he said softly, but firmly. He gently pushed Jeff down and onto the floor. "Stretch out here," Rusk said. Jeff, in all his hugeness, complied and stretched his body on the floor. "Breathe," Rusk said.

"Just breathe." Jeff kept his eyes closed and Rusk placed his hand over Jeff's head as if he were a conjurer, and intoned a mantra. "You breathe deep," Rusk said. "Breathe deep."

"Oh, God," Jeff said, and Polly saw that he was letting go. She had no idea what it was that he was letting go, but Jeff seemed like someone whose bones had suddenly given up their resistance to their flesh, as if the flesh were fluid and transparent and as if the soul were suddenly opaque and intensely radiant. Jeff sighed a deep sigh and Rusk, kneeling from above and behind Jeff's head, reached down to cradle his neck and slowly kneaded the huge muscles of his shoulders. "Inspire," Rusk said. "Breathe," he said. And Jeff's body seemed less gross, less commanding, and more like the body of a man whose heart had–after a period of absolute pause–begun to beat again, but now in a rhythm that seemed more tuned to the incoming waves of the sea, more tuned to the rhythms of the earth, and more resonant with those around him. "The flesh," Rusk said with his hands cupped around the back of Jeff's neck, "is only a sign. Not who you are. Your flesh is your resistance to the world."

And in a matter of seconds, Jeff abandoned his resistance to the world and seemed, for the first time since Polly met him, to be *of* this world, to be of the same world as Madeleine and as Kate had been. And now Polly felt that all had not been lost, that the love Madeleine needed might truly come from this man whom Rusk had, through an ageless ritual of touch, brought back from a terrifying experience of death.

The Menehune

Before she married Ben Toshi, the golf pro, Connie Nahiya was a stunning beauty living in a ramshackle house with whitewashed walls and exposed two-by-fours. The house had two bedrooms, a small kitchen, and a cool shaded veranda with rusted metal lawn chairs that squeaked when you rocked back and forth on them. Small as it was, the kitchen had an electric range, a refrigerator with a huge coil on top, and a round table for breakfast, lunch, and dinner. The cabinets were fashioned out of sturdy plywood by Connie's grandfather, and while they were rough-hewn and sometimes left splinters in her fingers, all the mis-matched dinnerware and the pots and pans, cups and glasses, fit nicely into their dark interior. Connie lived there with her mother Suki and with her great-grandmother Mama Pa'ele. Pa'ele was a nickname that stuck with her because she was so dark-skinned that late at night when the house was unlighted and she sat shriveled and unmoving on the one soft chair on the veranda, she was totally invisible.

No one knew how old Mama Pa'ele was, but one story that Connie heard when she was a child was that Mama Pa'ele had been a handmaiden to Liliuokalani when she was made Queen in 1891. At that time Mama Pa'ele was said to be as beautiful as a black sea pearl and sat on the back of a ceremonial sculpture of a dolphin in a fete honoring the elevation of the princess. If the story were true, then she would have to be more than one hundred years old.

When Connie was growing up, Mama Pa'ele would sing songs to her in the evening, and she would make a palaoa palai pancake for breakfast. Sometimes she would grind macadamia nuts into the mix and then caramelize the residue from crushed sugarcane. Mama Pa'ele had no teeth at any time that Connie could remember, and as far as she knew she had never seen a doctor, but Mama Pa'ele used to say that the joy of eating would keep her well and that as long as she possessed that joy, she would stay in the world she loved, sitting on the veranda, squeaking her lawn chair, staring into the distance where strange automobiles thundered by under the shadow of the volcano. The lawn had overgrown long since, and even from the elevation of the veranda, it was not easy to see over the scrub papaya and the scraggly monkeypod trees that now sapped much of the view she had seen as a young woman.

Grandfather had cut an old monkeypod tree to the ground long before Connie was born and he had fashioned a number of tools from it as well as a set of wooden plates and bowls, spoons and cutting boards, all of which still existed, and all of which saw good service throughout the year. For Mama Pa'ele, the monkeypod was a tree of trees.

But in recent years, Mama Pa'ele had grown silent. She sat staring into space on her green lawn chair. Her dark hair, showing signs of gray, but nonetheless preternaturally black, became a rat's nest over the years, and her grand-daughter Suki had given up trying to untangle it. Every so often, at an extreme of impatience, she would threaten to cut it off, and Mama Pa'ele would react with terror, and shrink back into the darkest corner she could find.

Connie had boy friends who would ask to come to the house, but she would try to keep them away. She would meet boys at the movies or at the state park or down at the ABC, but it was rare that she would let boys come to her house. They would come and see Mama Pa'ele sitting, looking into a world that had disappeared, rattling an imperfect rhythm in her chair, so small as to be mistaken for the mythical menehune, those tiny people who had disappeared from the islands a thousand years ago.

When Connie was a freshman at the community college training to be a dental hygienist, she began dating a young haole boy with luscious blonde hair and radiant blue eyes. He had perfect teeth and fragrant breath. His name was Parker Straus and his father owned a small gift shop not far from the Butterfly Inn in Kurtistown. What she liked about him was his slow, rhythmic way of walking and the sudden explosion of laughter when she told him something funny.

Parker had a ten year old car, a Mustang, with a special shift that he tried to explain to her, but her interest in cars was limited to their ability to get her where she wanted to go. Her personal problem with the Mustang was that the back seat was hardly large enough for them both, so their romantic evenings were limited to chaste necking in the darkest section of the local cinema-four.

Parker had taken her out one April evening when they both had a break from their academic pressures and after seeing the late showing of *Jurassic Park* at the student center, they drove up Route 11 above Mountain View. They stopped in an old farmers' road not far from the macadamia groves. The sky was clear. They could see the big dipper close to the horizon and the moon was such a sliver that the car was almost lost to view. They didn't say much to each other, but leaned across their respective bucket seats and began kissing, his minty tongue deep in her mouth. After a few awkward moments, Connie insisted they get out of the car and just walk a few paces in the woods. Parker saw no point in that, but he took her hand into the seclusion of an orchard and kissed her. When Connie detected his enthusiasm she decided not to let the moment pass. He reached for her breast and she touched him inside his trousers, but somehow it was not the way she wanted their lovemaking to be. Parker was a sweet and decent boy and quite different from the boys she had dated in high school who were impatient, crude, and in some ways basically misogynistic. She felt him pulling her to the ground, but she resisted.

"No, no," she said. "Not on the ground here. Too hard, too dirty."

And the back seat of the Mustang was so small his feet would be out the window. So she decided to take him home. Suki spent the weekend up in Waimea with Connie's sister Laura, who had just had her third baby and needed help. Mama Pa'ele would have gone to sleep long ago. Connie thought of the comfort of her own large bed. She was certainly not going to behave like a middle-schooler and let Parker take her on a stony bed of grass where she couldn't see his body and where their discomfort would mean they'd have no time to savor their mutual delights.

"We're not that far," she said. "No one's home, and it will be much nicer."

Parker backed down the twisty road and headed to Connie's house. He had been in only one or two of the old-fashioned Hawaiian houses that stood, like Connie's, without the conventional details of insulation, wallboard, and wall-to-wall carpeting. She warned him that it was a simple place, but she thought that in the dark, and under the circumstances, he was not likely to notice much by way of his surroundings.

Connie went into the house first and made sure her mother was gone. A weak night-light illuminated the one bathroom, but otherwise the house was silent and dark. Parker came in and walked on tiptoe into Connie's bedroom and sat on the bed. Connie went to the bathroom and came out to find him with his shirt off. "Where are you?" he said softly.

She stretched out on the bed next to him and they began kissing and fondling one another. She had loosened her blouse so as not to lose any buttons but he still had trouble trying to undo her bra. He asked her to move so he could get a better purchase, but in moving she hurt his arm and he squealed. He struggled with the catch until she pulled his hand in front and guided him to the snap between the

133

cups. Once the bra was off he touched her tentatively then kissed her breasts while she negotiated the zipper in his jeans. They twisted on the bed, he kicking his shoes off, she forcing his belt undone and then pulling his pants down while he shuffled his legs in an effort to free himself as if he were struggling with his clothes in a swimming pool. His mouth was on her left breast and his sex in her warm hand when they heard a soft gurgle that could not have come from outside the house.

They stopped and heard their breathing close to each other's ears. For a long moment they were statues. Not a sound. She squeezed her hand and he moaned very softly and drew in a breath and they heard the gurgle again. Connie sat up, now completely naked. Mama Pa'ele had to be asleep in her room. But she hadn't checked to see. Now that her eyes were adjusted to the dark, she rose quickly and opened Mama Pa'ele's door and stared inside. Her mother's bed was, as she expected, quite empty. But so was Mama Pa'ele's.

Back in her room, Parker's pasty body was almost aglow in the dark. Somewhat less visible, she looked around the room and was shocked to see very dimly that Mama Pa'ele was curled like a house-pet in her old brown camp chair deep in the corner of the room. Her eyes glistened slightly in the reflection of the night light as it shone on her bedroom door and into the room. Mama Pa'ele had been watching them all the time.

"Put on your clothes," she told Parker. But when he rose to meet her his erection was so profound that in the dark she let him enter her moistened vagina and she clutched at him as she caught her breath. They made love intensely standing up, hardly able to control their anxiety, and when they finished they fell slowly to the bed, separating after moments of sweaty groping.

Finally, Parker reached around in the dark for his clothes and took them out into the kitchen. Connie went into the bathroom and washed herself and tried to think of something to say to Mama Pa'ele. What had she seen? Did she understand any of it? And how much noise had she made while Parker had held her bottom firmly to his body and brought her to the pitch she had longed for?

When she came back into her room, she looked for Mama Pa'ele, but the camp chair was empty. Connie thought that it may have been a hallucination on her part, an impossible mistake, but Mama Pa'ele was definitely not in her room either. Parker spoke softly in the kitchen and while he spoke, Connie heard the rusty squeak of the lawn chair on the veranda. "What in God's name was that?" he asked.

"What did you see?"

"This tiny dark thing, a dwarf or a gnome. It skittered through the kitchen and out there," he said, pointing to the veranda. "What was it?"

"Mama Pa'ele," she said. "My great-grandmother."

"Lord, it was really a person?"

"Yes, of course."

"Did she see us?"

"She was right there in the corner near my closet. She was wide awake looking at us."

"How come you didn't know she was there?"

The next morning Connie waited for Mama Pa'ele to get up, but she slept late. Connie went down the road to get the newspaper and breakfast makings. Suki had run out of eggs and muffins. Left on her own, Mama Pa'ele would have had peanut butter and berry jam on white bread, but when Connie was home in the morning she scrambled eggs and toasted English muffins. Mama Pa'ele's days of making pancakes were long past, but her appetite never dimmed. Connie brewed some kona coffee in the percolator and sat down with the paper to read the want ads. She was interested in keeping track of job offerings in the dental line, just in case she might get a useful lead that would help after graduation.

Mama Pa'ele got up around eleven and scurried into the bathroom, then back to her room and appeared at the table looking hopeful. Connie greeted her and looked at her closely. There was no telling what she saw or what she thought, so she did not quiz her or ask her whether she noticed she had brought a friend home. "You sleep okay?" she asked. Mama Pa'ele nodded once. "I'm making eggs."

Connie broke the eggs into the buttered fry pan and swirled them around with her fork. She toasted the muffins in the oven, and put coffee in front of Mama Pa'ele. It might be possible that Mama Pa'ele had been asleep, even if her eyes were open. Perhaps she could not see in the dark. It was very unlikely that she heard anything. Usually Connie touched her arm before she began talking so as to get her attention and avoid having to repeat what she said. Because she rarely spoke, it almost went unnoticed that she communicated almost entirely in gesture and nod.

Connie took care of Mama Pa'ele as she usually did on Sunday. They ate their three meals together and Mama Pa'ele sat on the veranda listening to an old Emerson radio playing Hawaiian surfing music while Connie studied for the following day's courses. She saw Parker after school on Monday and listened to him tell her how weird it was to think someone was in the room with them. Connie told him that Mama Pa'ele had little or nothing to say at the best of times, and that she had indicated nothing that would suggest she had seen much of what went on. Basically, the only thing that worried Parker was that it might have been a little kinky.

Suki had come back to work at the ABC and took over caring for Mama Pa'ele. Connie thought that if Mama Pa'ele had seen anything she would have told Suki and that Suki would surely bring it up. The best thing Connie could do was to keep quiet. She went to school all week long, staying late to study in the tiny library with other girls in her classes, and saving time for a quick dinner with Parker. On the weekend, when Suki went back to Laura's with a bundle of supplies, Connie waited until dark and brought Parker home with her. She studied the house very carefully this time and warned Parker not to make noise. Suki was definitely gone and Mama Pa'ele was in her bed in the fetal position, a tiny bundle of sleeping flesh.

Parker was more adept this time with Connie's blouse and bra. He slipped out of his clothes quickly and silently knelt on the bed waiting with his arms out for her when she came from the bathroom. Connie slowed him down and helped him find the right way to touch her and when they actually made love it was much better than that first night. She was glad that Parker was such a quick study, and she felt very lucky to have chosen him over the other young men she could have had. His sweetness, his kindness, and even his essential shyness were not always the markers of a good lover.

When they finished, Connie rolled on top of Parker and kissed him. Then, she looked around the room, checking carefully each corner to see that it was not only dark, but empty. Parker kissed her and stroked her belly and then her back and they held each other side by side until they slowly drifted to sleep.

Connie woke to feel Parker warming her thigh with his erection. It was hours later and the bed sheets had fallen to the floor. They found themselves again breathless and caught up in their excitement. When they were finished, Connie heard the soft, but distinct gurgle that told her Mama Pa'ele was in the room. She turned and saw her deep in the corner, the faint nightlight reflected from her eyes. She kissed Parker while pressing her hand gently on his free ear, hoping that he may not have heard the sound. She felt his hands enjoying her body and she held him close to her until he fell back to sleep.

The room was empty in the morning, except for Parker,

sleeping quietly beside her. Connie decided she wanted him there with her when it became light, despite the fact that he would see how simple and homespun her house was. With Parker she did not have to pretend, nor did she have to be ashamed. He was willing to take her as she was, and that was good enough for her.

She got up first and went into the shower and waited for Parker to join her. They laughed a bit but restrained themselves and concentrated on washing and shampooing each other. When they were dressed they found Mama Pa'ele sitting in the kitchen with an impassive expression. A fresh pot of coffee was waiting for them.

Connie made them all some breakfast. Parker nodded to Mama Pa'ele and said, "Good morning." He looked at her with some curiosity at first, then saw a slow smile form on her lips. Mama Pa'ele met his eyes only for an instant, then looked down into her coffee. Parker looked over at Connie, who had seen it all.

"Are you all right, Mama Pa'ele?" she asked.

Mama Pa'ele nodded and took a piece of toast from the plate Connie offered her. When the breakfast eggs came, she hovered eagerly over her plate. Connie wanted to ask Mama Pa'ele whether she had seen them making love, but asking such a question was completely ridiculous. How could she ask her great-grandmother such a thing? It was always possible that she saw nothing. No one knew how good her eyesight was nowadays, and if it was as defective as her hearing, then perhaps there was no reason for her to ask any questions at all of Mama Pa'ele.

Parker and Connie sat over their coffee after Mama Pa'ele went out on the veranda and began rocking in the lawn chair. "I think she likes you," Connie said.

"She's so tiny. I don't think I've ever seen anyone that tiny. Like the Menehune who built the wall in Kauai. You ever think of that?"

"That's what my grandfather called her sometimes. Maybe

that's what she is. She's never been very big, but she's even got smaller since I was little."

"You get the feeling you could pick her up and have her sit on your hand."

"Not quite. But she is small."

"She doesn't talk at all."

"No. But she knows what she wants and knows how to make herself understood. She used to sing and talk when I was little. She told me stories about Pele and other gods and goddesses all the time. And she used to take me down to the park and then walk along the beach and we'd sing songs back and forth. These days I don't know what she thinks. I don't know what she imagines."

"She hasn't told your mother?"

"No. I'm sure my mother would say something."

"But it's weird. I don't know."

Mama Pa'ele turned on her Emerson radio and listened to music and took her food at the table with Suki and sometimes with Connie throughout the rest of the semester. On the weekends Suki apologized for having to be with Laura and the babies, but it was clear that Laura needed the help. Her husband, Tivi, worked a late shift during the week and on weekends tried to get some rest. With all the children under foot, that was no easy task. Suki got along well with Tivi and she simply doted on her grandchildren.

Connie brought Parker home on the weekends. They usually waited until after a film, or after they had done their schoolwork, and came in on Friday night when it was dark and Mama Pa'ele was asleep. They would creep into Connie's bedroom and make love and have breakfast in the morning with Mama Pa'ele. Parker said they should lock the bedroom door, but since there was no lock and since it opened outward instead of inward, they could not block the door. So they took their chances.

139

Some evenings, they were completely undisturbed. But there were also evenings when Connie would wake in the darkness and know that Mama Pa'ele was in the room with them. She made hardly a sound, but it was clear that she had entered some time in the night and that she sat waiting in the dark, sometimes silent, sometimes gurgling softly. Connie wanted to know what she thought of what they were doing, but she had no way of asking. It was always possible that Mama Pa'ele just came in to have their company. In her own room she slept with Suki, so it was not unreasonable to think that she may have awakened at night and felt lonely. Perhaps she noticed nothing of what was going on at all. However, Connie suspected that she must have understood exactly what they were doing. Maybe she liked watching them.

"She must know what we're doing," Parker said to her one weekend.

"Not necessarily."

"Why, because she never did it?"

"Because she may be a little blind."

"She smiled at me again this morning. At least I think it was a smile. She's got so many wrinkles you can't be sure."

"It was a smile. She likes you."

"Well . . . ."

"I mean it. You can tell when she likes someone. She was really sweet to me when I was little."

"She's the little one now. And so dark. Does it hurt your feelings if I call her very dark?"

"She's the black pearl. She's always been the black pearl."

"Because she's so black?"

"Because she's so beautiful."

Near the end of the term, Connie had made a remarkable lover out of Parker. She experienced orgasm every night they made love, and sometimes they even came together. Parker seemed not to see Mama Pa'ele when she came silently into her corner and watched them. She was never there in the morning when the light came up, and Connie was unaware of just how many hours Mama Pa'ele would spend in her bedroom. Each weekend morning Mama Pa'ele had the coffee ready in the percolator, and each morning she enjoyed breakfast with her and Parker. She appeared to take a keen interest in their conversation, even when Parker and Connie discussed academic matters that were quite foreign to her. They had become a curious little family.

Parker seemed content, seemed to have adapted to this odd arrangement until one night the week before final exams, when Mama Pa'ele grew discontented with her seat in the dark and clambered into the bed with them while they were naked and asleep. They had made love in many rich and different ways, and Connie was reveling in a wildly erotic dream involving coition on the wing, the way she imagined the golden mamo birds might do it.

"Jesus," Parker said, turning suddenly and waking her.

"What?"

"Look," he said, pushing back at her. He pushed so hard, she rolled off the bed onto their shoes on the floor.

Connie tried to get up, but Parker was out of the bed and stepping over her on his way into the kitchen before she could rise on one knee. When she got up she saw Mama Pa'ele dark against the sheets curled into a fetal position the way she often slept. She was snoring very quietly, oblivious to Parker's shock.

In the kitchen, Connie heard Parker pulling on his clothes.

"Parker, where are you going?"

"I can't deal with this," he said, anxiety raising the timbre of his voice. "She's right there curled up next to me. Jesus."

She stood next to him in her nakedness and kissed him, but felt his reluctance.

"I gotta go."

"Will I see you?"

Parker nodded vaguely and was out on the veranda moving quickly to the Mustang. She could barely see him among the trees but watched the lights of his car swivel down the drive and onto the road and away. She felt a sense of loss that she knew was permanent. She had lost a lovely young man.

Connie spent the rest of the night tossing in Suki's bed. There was no reason to wake Mama Pa'ele. She had gone into her bedroom to put a cover over her tiny body, then tried to go back to sleep herself.

She got through her exams with very good results. She saw Parker several times, but they did not share a meal or a serious talk. Parker made it clear in several ways that he could not continue their relationship. "You're great," he said, "but I gotta get my head together. I mean, something is weird if you know what I mean. I gotta concentrate on what I gotta concentrate on, so I'll see ya."

There was no point in pressing the issue. Connie did not want to talk about Mama Pa'ele with Parker. She really had nothing to say. Mama Pa'ele had climbed into their bed much the way a frightened or lonely child might climb into her parents' bed, seeking comfort and love. Parker found all this terribly strange and unnatural, but Connie had somehow come to terms with it and thought that in some cultures this might have been the most natural and loving way for people to behave. Connie had studied some anthropology and was willing to think about such things in more open ways than she imagined Parker could. And after all, Mama Pa'ele was her flesh and blood, the woman who sang to her when she was little and took her to the beach and pointed out the whales as they breeched in preparation for mating.

For her last semester at the community college, Connie spent her weekends alone in her room at night. For a few weeks after Parker left, Mama Pa'ele climbed into her bed on a Saturday night. But soon, she remained in her own room. Connie used the monkeypod salad dishes to make interesting salads with deviled eggs on the weekend, and Mama Pa'ele rubbed the soft wood with her fingers as if molding it into a convenient form. And near the end of Connie's last semester, Mama Pa'ele's appetite began to wither. She watched Connie with a sad, touching expression. When she went out on the veranda the metal lawn chair no longer squeaked. All Connie could hear while she studied was the soft susurrus of the monkeypod trees. Her last semester was her best, and after she put on her bright blue academic cap and gown and received her certificate, she found a good job with Dr. Kagawa in downtown Hilo.

When Mama Pa'ele died, Connie thought of calling Parker to tell him about the funeral, but she decided he would not come. By that time she had gotten over Parker and knew he was not really for her. Despite their eagerness and their success as lovers, she did not love him and he did not love her. It had been the first true romance for both of them, and she knew they had been good for each other. But it was over, and Connie needed to look ahead and find a man who would really make her happy. She thought about that when she was given the assignment of cleaning Ben Toshi's teeth the week before he went to Maui for the Mercedes Open.

Suki made the arrangements for Mama Pa'ele's funeral, which took place on a Tuesday morning in a light rain. Mama Pa'ele was buried in a child's black and gold casket with gilt handles and a crucifix in mother of pearl on the lid. It was very beautiful.

143

Why Not Live at the Hokele?

After college, Keezu Hanalima's advisor, Donald Orcott, set up an interview for him at the Hokele Hotel in Maui, where Keezu's old girlfriend, Lula Makahila worked the desk. Before going to Kapalua, he spent two days at his old haunts down on Front Street, drinking beer with Kurtzy Mendonça and Pereira Gomes, surfing buddies from Hanalei who were now whale watching in Lahaina. Kurtzy got some money when his grandfather died, enough to buy himself an old tub that was good for chasing the humpbacks, but not much more. With the boat as collateral, he took out a loan of thirty thousand dollars for a berth on the pier.

"A bargain," he said.

Pereira said he'd like to do the same thing himself, but as he told Keezu, holding on to money in Lahaina was tough right now.

Kurtzy put Keezu up in his place, two small rooms over one of the art galleries on Dickenson Street. Kurtzy kept a futon for friends and Keezu arrived with a case of Coors. He knew how to make himself welcome.

"You wanna work on the whale boats?"

"I don't know, man. I went down to the pier and thought about it. I like the hustle, you know. But I don't know if I need the shit. I listened to some of those people waiting with their tickets in their hands and I don't know. The kids'd drive you nuts. Some good lookin' women, though."

"Shit yeah. But they are cold, bro. You look at those yellow hairs. They are cold mothers."

Pereira opened three cans of beer and gave one to Keezu.

Kurtzy picked up the phone and ordered two large pies with double cheese, pepperoni, and mushrooms from Pizza Paradiso. When the order came they were on their third beer each. Pereira dug in first, and Keezu followed him. They burned their lips with the hot pizza, but they all laughed it off. "Man, this is cool. Where you livin'?" Keezu asked Pereira.

Pereira's girlfriend was the hostess at the Yacht Club on Front Street. So he lived with her way back on Lahainaluna Road in a small house tucked in among the lehua trees.

"It's a fucking jungle," Kurtzy said.

"It's okay," Pereira said.

The next morning Keezu nursed a minor hangover and went along with Kurtzy and Pereira on the whale watch starting at nine a.m. The customers crowded the staging area on Wharf Street. About thirty of them had tickets for the Sea Horse, Kurtzy's boat. Kurtzy wore a sea-captain's hat, a red bandana beneath it, cocked pirate-wise, and a blousy shirt that gave him a rakish look. He was such a big man that no one would mistake him for anything but the captain of the ship. Pereira, by contrast, was skinny and shorter than Keezu. When they got under way, Pereira took up the public address mike and began his routine about the history of Lahaina during the great whaling years. Then he described the humpback whales they were likely to see and gave everybody a pep talk about how lucky they'd be if they actually got to see one breech anywhere near them. "Some are as much as fifty feet long and weigh up to thirty tons. And you can hear them sing if you listen real close."

Keezu leaned on the gunwale, looking back at the receding harbor. He liked seeing the whales when they slammed their flukes down on the water like giants clapping. The people on the boat jostled each other, aiming binoculars and cameras out toward Kahoolawe, still distant. Kurtzy admitted that he never knew where the whales would be, so he watched the other boats closely. When they spotted whales, Kurtzy took off after the boats. One way or another, he always got his folks in for a good view when there was a view.

Pereira explained how the whales strained the plankton through their baleen, how the tongue weighed almost a ton, sometimes more, and how the humpbacks came here to mate and also to give birth. Keezu had heard it all before, but it was nice to see Pereira commanding the attention of all these people in their pastel shirts and hats. They seemed so carefree, so pleased with themselves. Keezu sometimes wished he could be just like them. But today he was glad he would never be mistaken for one of them. The whales played hide and seek. Keezu stared out to port when everyone on the starboard side suddenly shouted at a sighting, and he turned and saw nothing more than a splash of water far away. Pereira kept the anticipation high, but he also warned people that they would be lucky to get a good view of any whale today. The humpback sometimes liked to lift right out of the water and somersault back in, but the odds of seeing that, he told everyone, were more than 20 to 1.

They saw only two or three rising flukes all day long, and Keezu listened to the complaints of several tourists from California. They said they saw more whales from the freeway outside San Diego than they saw here. And they didn't have to pay money for it.

Lula sounded a little suspicious when she heard his voice. "This really is Keezu?"

"Yeah. It's me."

"You sound different."

"I'm a new man. Getting my act together. I been seeing Kurtzy and Pereira. They're whalers now."

"That's nice."

"I thought I'd come visit. You hooked up with one of those rich dudes?"

"I'm not hooked up with anybody," she said. He thought he

heard a reproving note in her voice.

"Me neither. So I thought I'd come up and try to locate you. What's a good day?"

"I'm working."

"Well, I meant after work. We could go out, you know?"

"Sometimes I work at night."

"Well tell me the best night. I'm just staying with Kurtzy and I can come up when it's good for you."

"I'm not sure you're all that good for me any time."

"Oh, man, don't be that way. I changed a lot since we were tight. I figure you did too, so how's about it? I have to come up there for an interview on Friday. Can I see you tomorrow?"

Lula surprised Keezu. He thought she'd be excited to see him. It had been what? Maybe two years. That was enough to get over their problem, that mistake with the mainland girl in Haena--something he did on a whim. And something he regretted.

Kurtzy loaned him his old Chevy pickup. Keezu thought he'd have to hitch up Route 30 the way he used to do in the old days, but Kurtzy came through. So Keezu drove up in the late afternoon and stopped at the Napili Market to buy some flowers for Lula. He thought about getting some Coors, but held back. He wanted to make a good impression.

Lula lived in a small condo back from the beach with three other girls in Napili Bay. He had a bit of trouble finding the place, but it was near the Bay Course with a view of the Bay Club Restaurant. When he finally got there, she was sitting in the living room with a book on her lap. She didn't get up for him, just called him in and folded the book slowly as he brushed himself off and held out the bouquet.

"I thought you might like some flowers," he said. He had practiced his opening line several times, but when he saw Lula and realized how much she had changed in three years, he forgot everything he'd prepared.

"Thanks."   She got up and took the flowers and found a Chinese vase. She put the flowers in the water and arranged them so they looked terrific. Keezu stood there feeling very awkward, but also very admiring.

"You got a nice place."

"Expensive," she said. "I've got roommates."

"Yeah, I'm with Kurtzy until I get a job."

"Okay."

"I'm interviewing at the Hokele. You like it there?"

She looked at him and gave him a reproachful laugh. "They pay good," she said.

"You're on the desk, right?"

"I went to school, so they started me on nights. Now I'm on regular hours. Except I have to fill in on some weekends. Everybody does that."

"You look real good."

"So do you, Keezu. You look a lot like your daddy."

Keezu's mother told him the same thing, but he didn't believe it. His daddy was a foreman in the sugarcane fields and had stark white hair. He also had fifty pounds on Keezu and smelled of cigars.

Lula had filled out a little and looked like she was in the movies. Her black hair glistened and her high cheekbones caught a bit of the sun's dying rays.   Her eyelashes were longer than he remembered, and her way of carrying herself implied an attitude of confidence that was new to Keezu. Her manner was independent, even a touch regal at moments. She stepped back to admire the flowers and offered him a hint of a smile. "That's nice," she said.

They went out in Lula's Mazda to the Orient Express for the chicken stir fry. Keezu was careful to order just one beer. He didn't have a lot of money and he was unsure what to do when Lula took the check and paid with her Mastercard. "You don't have to do that."

"It's okay, I'm the one with a job," she said. "I come here all the time."

"It's an okay place."

It took them a little while to get loosened up. Lula seemed more relaxed than he felt She didn't bring up the Haena incident. He was afraid she might, but she was cool. She talked about her roommates and about her job checking people in and checking them out. They came from everywhere. She had two families from Washington just yesterday. People came from Tokyo, from Paris, from Rome, from Toronto, from Madrid. And they came with so much luggage that at first she almost gasped. And after she got used to seeing the baggage filling the carriers, she was tempted to laugh. "But you never do that," she told him. "There's a whole set of rules you follow. And we go through additional training. It's a science, I suppose you could say."

He surprised Lula by telling her he'd taken the hospitality course at Kauai Community College and was recommended to the Hokele. He knew that the Hokele was impressive and that if he could get a job, the tips would be pretty impressive, too. "I almost backed out of the interview because you worked here. I didn't know how you'd feel." He didn't get a reaction. "Maybe I should try the Kapalua Bay Hotel."

"Don't let me stop you. The Hokele is a big place and they do a lot of hiring."

"You'd be okay with that?"

"Question is, would *you* be okay with that?"

He wasn't sure what she meant. "Yeah, I suppose so. If I get the job, that'd be great."

The next day Keezu drove the old Chevy down Office Road into the turn-around in front of the Hokele and saw one of the young men in his light tan uniform come up to valet park his truck. "No, man. I'm suppose to talk to Mr. MacDougall. For a job. Where should I put this?"

The parking attendant didn't seem irritated. "I'll show you." He pointed to a side road where some dark green landscaping trucks stood in the shade. He put his truck behind them and went down the long walkway, lush with bushes and low trees. He passed a hedge of yellow flowering hibiscus, some brilliant anthrum, and massive red ginger flowers. The cool ocean breeze came to him through the body of the hotel. He looked out through the lobby at the distant sea. The sun was behind him and the light flooded the water in a different way than it did in Lahaina. People paid a lot of money for this view. Maybe it was worth it.

Lula was not at the desk when he asked for Mr. MacDougall. The office was downstairs behind the Kapukapu Lounge. It was larger than Kurtzy's apartment. Big paintings of sailboats hung on the walls and behind the desk he saw a row of awards and diplomas. "Are you available right now?" Mr. McDougall asked. Keezu nodded. He watched Mr. McDougall reviewing his transcript. It said that he graduated the program, so his not having his Associates diploma with him wasn't that crucial. Fortunately, Mr. MacDougall knew Keezu's advisor. "You know any native dances?" Keezu stared at him, uncertain what he meant. "Like they do at the luaus?"

"You have luaus here?"

"Sometimes. I just wondered if you knew any of the dances."

Keezu was still mystified. "I seen some dances, but I don't know them myself."

"Ah, I thought you might. You've got a dancer's body."

Keezu laughed. "Me?"

"Sure. You've seen the Polynesian dances, haven't you? You'd be perfect."

Jimmy O'Brien trained Keezu for the first three days on the job. Keezu was taken on as a bellman. Jimmy was stiff at first. He was a red-head, short and muscular. He was older than Keezu and the first thing he said to him was, "You're lucky to get this job. You got some connections, maybe?"

"Not really," he said. "I mean I went to school and all, but I don't know anybody if that's what you mean."

"I tried to get a job for a buddy of mine and they turned him down. It kind of pissed me off."

"You pissed at me?"

Jimmy shook his head. "No, you're okay." Then Keezu told him he needed a place to stay until he got some money aside. "Why not live at the Hokele?" Jimmy said with a grin. He explained how they had kept a barracks down out of sight of the guests and for a small sum Keezu could bunk in there. "Lot of guys do it. Then you get out when you're ready."

Keezu moved in and gave Kurtzy back his pickup. He hitched a ride with two kids driving up to play golf at the Bay Course. They were just kids, but they seemed to have plenty of money. They talked about where they'd played golf and where they were going to play when they got home. They seemed to take golf very seriously. They talked about back nines and three-putting and sand traps most of the way up the highway. They asked Keezu questions about the courses they wanted to play, but when they found out Keezu didn't play golf, they didn't have a lot to say to him. They just let him off at the entrance to the course and Keezu walked the rest of the way to his digs.

When he got to work, he thought most of the guests might be Japanese, but actually they were from Canada. He took a family of very tall Canadians up to their room and stacked their luggage where they told him to and got five dollars Canadian from the father. "If you need me, just ask for Keezu."

"Keezu," the wife said. She was as tall as Keezu, brown haired, plain round face, but with a good figure. "Interesting name."

He could feel her looking at him as he left the room. Lula'd change the Canadian money for him at the desk, but he wished they'd give him American cash he could just put away. He had several more families to see to their rooms and then a couple from Georgia who seemed to be having a fight, but silently. Two women from Nova Scotia checked in and one of them told him how cute he was and the other laughed uproariously. "Janie thinks I'm a naughty girl."

"Oh, she is a naughty girl," the other said. "You better watch out."

The naughty girl gave him ten dollars American and held his hand for a second or two longer than necessary. Keezu began to think the job might not be that bad.

Keezu saw the naughty girl later that day. She was wearing purple shorts and a green tank top and looked pretty good. She was in the arty gift shop on the way to the restaurant. She was examining a large sculpture of a pair of dolphins soaring in air. What would she want with something like that? But she had the money, so who was he to worry about it?

"So, Keezu," she said when he came back up from the Kapukapu Room, after stacking a hundred dining chairs out of the way. "Should I buy that lovely sculpture or not?"

She must have seen him heading down the hallway earlier. She stood beside a large ship model framed against the wall. He wondered why she would ask him such a question.

"I mean, do you think they look like real dolphins, the way they come out of the water? I've got a perfect place for them."

"Sure," he said. "Yeah, they look good."

"Where can I get a drink at this hour?"

"Right around the corner. Out on the terrace." He walked a few steps, waiting for her to follow him. He pointed past the large oak table with the huge floral display. A few people sat outside. Inside two women huddled over an open laptop computer going over some papers. It was a balmy afternoon. The wispy clouds hung motionless over the water. "Right there," he said.

"You can't take my order? A vodka martini?"

"They got waitresses," he said.

Lula caught his eye as he went back to his station. He wasn't going to talk to her, but she signaled him, holding up a key card as if she had a job for him. "You gotta be careful of that."

"What?"

Lula smirked. "You know exactly what I mean."

"I didn't do anything? She wanted to know where to get a drink."

"Oh, Keezu," she mimicked, "how do I get a drink around here?"

Keezu looked down at his name tag. He heard a car door slam and saw another family coming in. He turned and grabbed the luggage cart and wheeled it out and loaded seven large suitcases and three huge golf bags. He took them down to a room very close to the water. The family was from New York and the man's name was Pankhurst. He gave Keezu a ten dollar bill and asked him how to get to the Plantation Course in the morning.

"We got a shuttle."

"You know, I need a box of Titleists. You think you could get me a box this afternoon?" He opened his wallet and took out two twenty-dollar bills.

Keezu wasn't sure he could do that, but he took the money and said he'd be back. Jimmy O'Brien said people did that kind of thing all the time. So Keezu took the shuttle himself and went up to the Plantation Course and had a look around. He was no golfer, but he did appreciate the views from up on the Plantation Course. The fairways were immense, rolling, perfect. He got good views of the water in several directions. He watched a few tall men in patterned trousers and white hats leaning their golf bags against the racks in front of the club house. They were tanned, about his age, and laughing.

He walked up the stairs on the left, into the clubhouse, then into the pro shop and found several different boxes of Titleist golfballs. "Which are the best?" he asked the short, older woman behind the counter. She pointed to one of the boxes. When he brought it over to her, he wondered if he got a discount because of his uniform. But apparently not. He took the bag she gave him, and the change, and started out.

"Your receipt," she called out to him.

He waited for the next shuttle and watched as several good looking women came in wearing hats that said "Ping" on them. They had big golf bags and they smiled radiantly at each other. They did not seem to notice him sitting there on the low wall waiting. He tried to imagine where they were from. He thought California for sure. While he sat there some men with deep maroon polo shirts and white golfing hats came and talked with them and after a short time they got two golf carts and moved off. In the distance he heard the solid whack of a long drive off the tee. Behind him he heard some greens keepers arguing.

When he got back Mr. Pankhurst was alone in the room. He had just taken a shower and came to the door in a white terrycloth robe. Keezu handed him the golf balls and the change. Mr. Pankhurst gave him the twenty-dollar bill back as a tip. "You play golf?" he asked.

"Not really."

"What's 'not really' mean? Not at all?"

"No, I mean I played once or twice."

"You ever play the Plantation Course? I've heard the eighteenth hole is a monster. You've got some kind of intense gully or something after your second shot. That right?"

"Actually, I never played the course. I don't know about it."

"You know . . . what's your name?" He squinted at the name tag. "Keezu. Yes, Keezu. You know, you've got to take golf a little more seriously. If you're going to get someplace in life. It's not just a game, you know. It's a philosophy. A kind of philosophy of life. It teaches you about how to be consistent, how to be powerful, how to focus all your attention on the object of your desire. Do you understand what I'm saying?"

"I think so."

"And it makes you a goal-oriented person. A man with a clear purpose and a clear sense of how he is going to get there. And it teaches him to know when he has reached his goal. And the rewards are immense. Self-satisfaction. That's the most important reward. You understand that? What I mean? Self-satisfaction? And then there is the admiration of others. I myself don't feel that is as important as other people say. I don't run it down, mind you. But it is not the ultimate. No, the ultimate is self-satisfaction. Knowing you did it yourself. And Keezu. This is important. Knowing you did it by the rules. You followed the rules. You understand what I am saying? Golf is life, Keezu. Do you follow the rules?"

"Sure. I mean, yeah. Like most of the time."

"It's got to be all the time, Keezu. You follow the rules and you will get ahead in life, and that's what I'm trying to tell you." He tore the wrapper off the box of Titleists and took out a smaller box with three golf balls in it. He handed it to Keezu. "I'm going to give you these golf balls, Keezu. This is a not a present. It's an investment in a young man's future. I want you to take these golf balls and get out on one of these incredible courses and start your training for the future. Follow the rules. Understand the meaning of getting to where you are going. And aim, I mean really aim, at producing in yourself the self-satisfaction that comes only with success. You can do it,

Keezu."

Keezu stood there with the small box of golf balls. "Okay."

"Get out there and begin at the beginning. That's what I tell my people. Start at the beginning and do not stop until you have reached your goal. The eighteenth hole. And watch out for all the sand traps in life. Not everyone is straight enough off the tee to avoid the messes and the roughs and the traps that hold us back. But if you are strong, Keezu. And if you are focused as intently as you need to be in this life, then you will straighten yourself out and you will reach your goal. Self-satisfaction," he said again, after a moment's staring into Keezu's eyes. "Have I made my point?"

"Yes sir."

"You know what I mean when I say you need to be goal-oriented?"

"Maybe . . . ." He wasn't sure what to say.

"What is your goal in life, Keezu?"

"My goal in life?" Keezu was uncertain. "I guess to have a good job, I suppose."

"You have a good job now?"

"I think so."

"And you follow the rules of this job?"

"Sure."

"From what I've seen of you, Keezu, you are doing a good job. You got us into this room and made us feel really welcome. That's not so easy when you've been traveling the way we've been. And then you got the Titleists for me and got me the right change. That counts, Keezu, that counts. How far you can go in this job depends on you."

"Right."

"So what is your goal? What goal have you set for yourself in this job?"

"To do a good job, I guess."

"No! Not just to do a good job. You do a good job no matter

156

what job you have. Your goal, Keezu, is to own the Hokele."

"Own the Hokele?"

"Of course. How do you think men come to own great hotels? You think it's given to them? You think it's handed to them? No. They take it, Keezu. They're like champions on the golf course. They look for their opportunity, then they make their charge. They put themselves in first place by planning and by strategy. Never do they lose sight of their goal. It's careful planning, saving their energy for the right moment, building day by day. Keeping your eye on that flag. Aiming at the flag. Do you save your money, Keezu?"

"Yes. Yes, I'm saving all my tips."

"Go without, Keezu. That's my first advice. At your age you can learn to go without. That way you can save more and if you save more and if you have a clear goal you can take that money and make yourself a wealthy man. Remember, there are many unhappy people in the world but if you have made yourself a wealthy man by following the rules and by setting your own goals, you will have not only happiness, but self-satisfaction. The greatest happiness comes from self-satisfaction. Believe me, Keezu. Make yourself a happy man. Save your money. Go without. And that way you will achieve self-satisfaction."

"Thanks," Keezu said, not knowing what else to say.

"Okay," Mr. Pankhurst said. He closed the door and Keezu walked back up to the lobby with the golf balls in his hand. Jimmy O'Brien was at his station.

"What took you so long?"

"You kidding? I had to wait for the shuttle. Then Mr. Pankhurst got me. He's an interesting guy."

"Yeah, well we got to set up some tables downstairs, so let's get on it."

On his day off, Keezu wondered what he should do. He wanted to talk with Lula, but she was working. He didn't have a car, and he wasn't sure he was supposed to hitch hike while he was working at the Hokele. So he decided to go down to Napili and find a beach to lie on. He was thinking about what Mr. Pankhurst had told him. He had no real goals that he could think of. What kind of goal could he figure for himself? When he thought back, he realized he had set himself the goal of getting work in the Hokele hotel on the island of Maui. And he achieved that goal. So was that like the first hole on a golf course? Maybe it was. But what was the second hole going to be? What should he aim for next? Thinking about it distressed him. He borrowed one of the hotel's surf boards and paddled out to the swells. The water was fine, but there were only a few small waves, and rather than ride them in, he lolled on his board and watched as some other surfers came and went. He felt good not having to run errands, not having to stack chairs, not having to move tables, and not having to hop to when a new family showed up. He realized his goal today was to learn how to do nothing.

In his third week on the job, Keezu looked into the box where he kept his tip money. He had $474.53. He put the money on his bedspread when he was alone in the 'racks, as the other two guys called it. He matched the twenty-dollar bills and the ten-dollar bills and the five-dollar bills and the one-dollar bills so they all faced forward. He thought of getting wrappers for the change, but he wasn't sure where you went for them. He kept his money locked under his bed, but he realized that he could lose it all if somebody came in and just stole the suitcase.

He felt a little stupid when he asked Lula what he should do with his money.

"Where do you cash your checks?" she asked him.

"The Hawaii bank in Kaanapali."

"So, do you have a savings account?"

"No."

"Well get one. Put your money in your savings account.

Then you'll know where it is and you get a report every month. They pay interest."

It all seemed so simple to Lula. "What's your goal in life?" he asked her.

"What kind of question is that?"

"That guy from New York, the one with all the golf bags. That's what he asked me. He told me my goal should be to own the Hokele." Lula laughed and he wished he hadn't told her. "I know it's stupid, but that's what he said."

"You think you're going to save enough money to buy the Hokele Hotel?"

"No, no. Come on. I just want to get my money working for me. I'm going to save all my tips so I can get a place of my own out here."

"Fine. Do it."

"So what's your goal?"

"To own the whole island," she said, and laughed again.

"Be serious. I mean it. You gotta have a goal if you wanna get somewhere."

"I'm where I want to get," she said. "I meet interesting people and I make my own living and nobody tells me what to do when I walk away from that desk. That's my goal. I don't want anyone telling me how I'm supposed to do things when I'm away from work. You don't think that's enough?"

"Yeah, I get your point. Thing is I don't like it when people tell me what to do when I'm off work or on work. But I never thought of it as a goal. How you supposed to get ahead with a goal like that?"

"I'm already ahead."

Keezu had a bank book that told him he had $732.16. He thought about how he could do without, but there was not much he really needed. So doing without meant he did not have to change his habits very much. He decided to stop drinking beer and see how much money he could save. But there was no way of telling. If he spent a certain amount each week on beer he could figure out just what he was saving, but it never worked that way. So he decided to follow some suggestions he read in *Money* magazine and set up a budget that included a certain amount for entertainment and then see if he could cut back.

It actually worked for a while. He set himself $45 a week for entertainment and spent $27.44 the first week. He put the $17.56 in the bank that week with his tips. He had $903.29. It felt good. He tried to shave a few dollars off some of the other items on his budget, and after a while he began to see that he could do without a good many things and save a few dollars at the same time. Trouble was, he didn't get out to see people the way he used to. He hadn't seen Kurtzy and Pereira for three weeks, mainly because they were expensive. They always wanted to go upstairs to the bar at Cheeseburgers in Paradise and toss down a few, then eat some burgers and toss down some more. Keezu could shoot the whole week's worth of entertainment right there. Instead, Keezu decided to set himself a goal of saving $2500 from his tips and from doing without. With that kind of money he could start to look around for a place to set down in. The 'racks were getting on his nerves.

In the second week of the second month, Mr. McDougall left a note at his station. He wanted to see him down in the office. Keezu suddenly got frightened. Had he done something wrong? He couldn't think of anything. Jimmy O'Brien hadn't complained to him about not doing this or that. Did one of the patrons say something about him? He looked at his uniform. It was clean. He was clean. As he walked downstairs he rehearsed in his mind all his recent conversations with people he'd hauled luggage for, but nothing special hit him.

"How you doing?" Mr. McDougall said. He shuffled some

papers on his desk. "Things going okay for you?"

"Okay. Sure. Real good."

"Jimmy says you're doing pretty well. You like the work?"

"Sure. Yeah."

"The barracks okay for you?"

"For now, sure."

"I fought for the barracks, you know. They didn't have that when I came here. They used the place for the gardeners. A big storage shed. I told them if we wanted to attract some good talent they might need to fix it up so people like you could get their start."

"That's good."

"I'm proud of that. Paid off, didn't it?"

Keezu nodded. He watched Mr. McDougall go over to the corner and haul out a large box. He put it next to his swivel chair and sat down. He made a rustling sound when he put his hand in and pulled out a woven headband of wide-blade grass.

"Sit down."

Keezu sat down.

"Know what this is?" Keezu shook his head. "It's one of my new ideas. I think you're going to like it." He held it up for Keezu to see.

"A headband? One of those ceremonial headbands?"

"Right. Here's my idea and here's where you come in. At night, when it starts to get dark, we've got these terrific torches that I've ordered. Tiki lamps. We put them up and down the walkway in the entrance, and out into the valet parking area and down and around the terrace restaurant." While he spoke he rooted around in the box and came up with two woven grass anklets and then pulled out a loincloth and short woven grass breeches. "I think it'd be smashing if you'd get dressed up in this native gear and take a flame, run from torch to torch, lighting each one, just at dusk. What an effect. And just in keeping with the island tradition. You know what I mean?"

Keezu took the anklets and studied them. Then he looked at the breeches.

"At dusk you get dressed up in this outfit and run from torch to torch. You want to run the way they do in the Olympics, you know? That way we connect to the idea of a great tradition. Island games and things like that. It will be very impressive." Mr. MacDougall put the gear back into the box and pushed the box over to Keezu. "The torches will be here next week and I'll have landscaping put them in. It all connects with Pele, the god of light."

"Pele?"

"Sure, the ancient Hawaiian god of fire and light."

"That's Pele?" Keezu asked.

"Sure. You want to brush up on your Hawaiian myths. Now, the thing is that you'll have to stay on a little later and come in a little earlier on the nights you light the torches. And I've worked it out in your favor so you get a little more on those days. You get an extra hour and a half, eighteen dollars each time you light the torches. It's not going to take you an hour and a half. Don't worry about that. With you running, it can't take more than about 20 minutes, probably less. And what an effect it will be. I see it now. Really classy."

Keezu looked down into the box.

"Now, what else can you think of to make this really authentic. I want it to be the real thing, the way the islanders used to do it before we came. You have some suggestions for island music that we could have on the PA system? Anything you suggest. I thought of Keili'i Reichel, but it could be anybody. I'll let you know when the torches are in place and when you can start. Okay?" He gave Keezu a big smile and stuck out his hand. Keezu shook it but he didn't know what he was shaking it for.

In the barracks, Keezu took the outfit out of the box and looked at it. What the hell was he supposed to do with this? He was supposed to be somebody doing some ritual like they did before the haole came here? What kind of shit was that? He called Lula and asked if he could come and talk with her.

Lula was home with one of her roommates, Karla Margolin. Karla was working on a jigsaw puzzle on a card table near the kitchen. "Why don't you let us see what you look like with it on?" Lula said. Keezu resisted the whole idea. "No, go ahead. Put it on. You get extra money? You could put that extra away, you know."

Keezu went into the turquoise bathroom and took off his clothes. The soap smelled of lavender, like the soap his mother used. He put on the breeches, then the anklets, then the crown and looked at himself in the mirror. He looked stupid. He didn't want Lula to see him, but she called him out.

"Hey," she said when he came out, "not bad. Nice bod."

Karla laughed. Then she said, "Lula's right. You look like the guys in the shows they put on in the hotels in Honolulu. A little skinnier maybe."

"This is supposed to be the native thing," Keezu said. He spread his legs and jumped up and down, making crude musical sounds.

"Well, you look like a native," Karla said.

"I am a native, mostly. But I can't see doing this. Running around lighting torches?" He turned to find a mirror in the living room and saw himself and Lula and Karla behind him. The crown on his head looked phony. He looked phony, even though he was the real thing. He couldn't do it. It didn't matter how much they paid him.

"What about your goals?" Lula asked when he got dressed again.

Keezu waited until the torches were in place. He took the box of woven garments downstairs and left them in Mr. McDougall's office and gave in his pass key and his barracks key and his name tag. He folded his uniform neatly and put it on top of the box and wrote a short note: "Sorry. I can't do it. Keezu." He went out on Route 30 early in the morning and picked up a ride with a woman who did bookkeeping for Bubba Gump's. She recognized him from having drinks in the Terrace. He told her he was visiting friends, but not that he was leaving the Hokele.

Kurtzy took him on the Sea Horse and gave him Pereira's old mike. Pereira was promoted to be the bartender and soda man. Kurtzy had the bright idea to put in an ice chest and to sell ice cream sticks, sodas, cold beer, and what have you. "You get pretty dry out there, bro," he said. Keezu learned the patter pretty quickly and did the job just about as well as Pereira had. There wasn't much to it, and he got bored by the third day, but there was something about being out on the water in the sunlight with the chance of seeing one of the great beasts lift out of the sea in front of you that suited him. The anticipation of the tourists was powerful and contagious, so no matter how many times he went out, he always had the feeling that he might see something he had never seen before. One of the tourists said something to him about being close to nature, and Keezu admitted there was virtue in that. Another tourist, a woman, talked to him about *Moby Dick* and said it would be especially interesting to him because of some character in the beginning who was like him. Keezu didn't plan on reading it.

He didn't see much of Lula. He and Kurtzy and Pereira threw a few down at Cheeseburgers in Paradise every couple of days or so. And Keezu, with the money he saved working at the Hokele, found himself a one-room place in view of the great Banyan tree in Courthouse Square. So life was okay. He thought now and then of the goals he should set for himself and Lula's words sometimes came back to him. He was where he wanted to be right now. He didn't need to get dressed up in a costume and he didn't need to think about running around almost naked for the amusement of people who never even heard of Pele. Right now he was feeling close to the whales, out of sight when he wanted to be, ready to show himself when people least expected it. He still had the three golf balls Mr. Pankhurst gave him, unwrapped, near his bed. He had no plans to take up golf but he thought maybe he had now reached hole number 2, the one with the water hazard.

Is God Calling You?

The Celestial Connection on Hanapepe Road faced the Cafe Espresso, a popular restaurant diagonally across the street. Julian Kusaka found a painter right there to transform the large glass windows of his storefront into an inviting shrine-like presence, very much in keeping with the relaxed atmosphere of the arty little town. Julian had been in advertising, but, as he told people, he was then a different person. He had seen God the way other people saw their way clear to buying expensive houses. God was there in front of him, a fact, a telling presence in his life. And Julian discovered his mission in life.

In one sense, none of this was strange. He had been a significant figure in local advertising in Honolulu, with offices downtown by the Ala Wai Canal near the Convention Center at Waikiki. For many years the work satisfied him, but his wife Lynn complained that he occasionally buttonholed friends at gatherings in their house and asked unusual questions, such as, "Where do you think we go when this life is done?" Such questions, she said, are appropriate in some circumstances, but at one a.m., when a friend stands by the door holding it open for his wife as they leave, it was an unlikely gambit.

Julian was a direct descendant of Portuguese missionaries who came to the Islands in the 1860s. His more immediate relatives were secular, but he still had his forebears' Bibles, Hymnals, and prayer books. It was in the blood, his wife told friends when they divorced. Something, she said, manic when it came to God, something that she never bargained for. What she had hoped for was a life of comfort and relative ease, the kind of life that they enjoyed when Julian was a fierce money-making businessman with a big house, two sporty cars, and a labrador retriever who once got lost for days near Likeke Falls. That was the life she had, the life she wanted, and the life she would not give up when Julian explained that God meant more to him than advertising.

Just how the transformation came about was difficult for Julian to explain, although he mentioned once to a friend that it began while he was talking to his dog, Wakea. Wakea was the most sincere being that Julian knew. Wakea looked deeply into his eyes as if making contact with his soul, and Julian relied on Wakea to listen to him as he spoke of his fears and his longings. Wakea never wavered, but always listened attentively and rested at Julian's feet like a guardian of the celestial gates. As he gazed into his soft brown eyes, the spiritual goals he sought seemed already to have been achieved by Wakea. He had never gazed into the face of a being more at peace with the world.

Among his ancestors' possessions were a few books in English, but most were Spanish or Portuguese. He often read Jeremy Taylor's *The Art of Holy Living* and *The Art of Holy Dying*, seventeenth-century books still in striking condition, considering the humidity in Honolulu. In reading these books–which Julian's wife declared the most dismal, depressing books she had ever seen–Julian began to think about the nature of God's love and God's expectations of him. He had come from pious people who lived respectful of the land and the water around the land. Such a heritage shaped him in ways that were mysterious to him. So it was not a total surprise that when he was fifty-five, he decided to leave the glitter of Waikiki and retreat to the simple life in Hanapepe.

He chose Hanapepe because it seemed at the time to be a remote village, one street, really, with a lifestyle vastly more tolerant than he was used to in Honolulu. Moreover, the dynamic quest for money and success was absent in Hanapepe. The dominant ethos, expressed in a genteel bohemianism associated with art and artists, suited Julian. It implied that if the spiritual needs of the community could be encompassed in the pursuit of art, that it would be only a slight extension to connect them to the quest for God.

The woman who painted his windows interpreted the garden of Eden in Hawaiian terms, with coral hibiscus, rainbow heliconia, catteleya orchids, bougainvillea, anthurium, kahili ginger, moth orchids, red collinsiana, and many more exotic and wonderful flowers whose colors virtually radiated through the glass. She painted Adam's face poking through a stand of plumeria on the left window, and Eve's face framed by a brilliant red 'ohi'a lehua bush on the right window. Over the doorway, extending the length of both windows, she painted "Is God Calling You?" with two cobalt telephone handsets, one on each end.

Inside the large room, Julian installed four benches, each of which could fit five people comfortably. He placed these facing forward, stretching from the right wall. On the left wall he had a carpenter build a shelf with five telephones, each in a different pastel tone. They were connected to machines hidden in the back of the store, next to the small kitchen and close to the unisex bathroom. The listener to the saffron phone heard Julian speaking of the nature of God and of the joys of spiritual excitement contemplating the eyes of a loved one. The violet telephone talked about the tears of Mary, the gold telephone spoke of the joyous laughter of the angels as they witnessed the resurrection of Lazarus.

Julian published a few small chapbooks of his thoughts about following a spiritual path. One of them was called, "Wakea's Gaze," and told the story of how he had looked into the heart of his best friend and knew that he must change his life. Wakea looked out from the cover, calm and pleased. Another, called "Suffering the Pain," told how Julian weathered the shock of leaving his old life and starting anew. He was careful not to involve his wife's reactions more than as a brief comment in passing, explaining that her path was in a different direction and that he wished her well. He did not mention in the chapbook that her lawyers had taken his house, half of his Keogh account, the two Mercedes 420s, and prevented him from withdrawing his interest in Ilima Advertising. As a result, he had very little ready cash, but because Lynn took over the business and kept it running, he was granted a stipend large enough to sustain him in Hanapepe. He also won custody of Wakea.

The woman who painted the storefront windows offered to make some paintings on religious themes and he accepted. She provided a painting for every telephone, each an emblem of its message. The first portrayed a Polynesian Jesus sitting on a rock, petting a dog that resembled Wakea. The second was a Polynesian version of the piéta, the third showed Jesus standing as his disciples moved the rock from Lazarus' grave. The fourth showed St. Paul's conversion on the road to Damascus. Strangely enough, he was riding a sea-turtle and the lightning struck the road in a grove of gigantic koa trees. The fifth interpreted St. John's four horsemen of the apocalypse. Each horse was actually a dolphin, each horseman a jockey, and the overall effect was more joyful than frightening. Julian felt all the paintings were upbeat and suggested the positive values he hoped others would associate with The Celestial Exchange.

During his first week, he sat at the desk installed against the back wall of the store. Wakea sniffed the new location and walked around its walls for a long time before pulling up next to the desk and stretching the length of his body on the cool floor. To accompany his two early publications, Julian decided to write a chapbook to place by each of the five telephones. He wrote the first for the Polynesian Jesus, and worked on the one for the Piéta. He had notes for the conversion of Paul, Lazarus, and the apocalypse. He felt a thrill of intense joy, almost a divine pain like that of St. Teresa as he looked around his white-washed chapel.

His first guest was a powerful-looking heavy-set local woman with a light blue T-shirt advertising her estrogen. She stepped inside and looked around. "Hi," she said. "Good phones. I've never seen those colors before."

"Try one," he said.

She took the violet phone beneath the piéta and listened for a few moments to Julian describing the pain of separation and the sense that all humans have of being somehow apart from God. She did not listen long enough to hear him discuss the ways in which separation can be repaired and how tears can turn to joy. "Was that you?" she asked.

Julian nodded.

"Good voice," she said. "Are these paintings yours?"

In one sense, of course, they were. But he answered, "No, a local artist did them. She has her work displayed across the street." He pointed to the left of Café Espresso.

"What are you selling?" she asked him.

"I'm not selling anything," he said, rising from his chair. "I'm interested in connections. Is God calling you?" he asked.

"I'm not sure," she said, and left. She seemed headed across to the art gallery. So he took solace in the thought that he may have facilitated a connection of sorts. Wakea rose and stood facing the door. He stared after the woman as if he expected her to return.

Through the rest of the week, people roamed through the space, picked up the telephones, sometimes one after another, and listened for a minute or two. Children came in with their parents and made a great deal of noise jostling with each other to get possession of the right color phone, but none of them listened for very long, and few listened at all carefully. Some people were curious about Wakea, especially after recognizing him in the painting and on the cover of the chapbook. Some people were curious about Julian. When they wanted to know how he had come to set up shop (their way of understanding what he was doing) here in The Celestial Connection, he gave them a copy of his chapbook with Wakea's portrait. When a few people asked him why he was here, he asked them the same question. "What are we all looking for?" he asked them. "What significance lies beneath the surface of everyday events? What gives true meaning to your life?"

Unfortunately, such questions ordinarily had the effect of intimidating the casual visitor, who left promptly after such questions. But by the third week, people who came through the door were more aware of what he was doing. He had finished his chapbook on Lazarus and had it printed and arranged next to the gold telephone. He was now working on St. Paul. The covers of each chapbook replicated the paintings above them. After having distributed only eighteen chapbooks in the first two weeks, Julian decided to charge two dollars for each one instead of giving them away. This strategy boosted distribution more than double. In the third week he sold forty-four chapbooks, and in the fourth week he sold almost a hundred. It was a principle he had learned in advertising: when you give it away it appears to have no value. When you price it right it flies off the shelf.

In the fifth week he found himself with a gathering of six people who had wandered in on Sunday expecting some kind of service. He was not quite prepared for such an event. Yet, he saw that they had arranged themselves on the benches as if they were pews. So, he decided that he would wait until eleven o'clock and offer them a few words. They seemed very pleased when he began talking about the nature of the spiritual journey.

"I am no preacher," he said, when he stood before them, "and this is not a church in any ordinary sense of the word. It is more like a chapel. I suppose that is as much as I would want to claim for it, but it is nonetheless a place that I think of as having a sacramental quality

171

to it. I am very glad you are here with me today, and I would like to give you space to offer your own prayers as you see fit."

When he finished, Wakea stretched, yawned, and settled down. He looked thoughtfully at the people sitting on the benches. The six sat quietly while two more curious people stepped in. They sensed the quiet and took a seat on the last bench. They were unclear as to why they were here and why they had sat down, but they were respectful and remained quiet.

It took Julian a few minutes to realize that the original six were waiting for some kind of closure. Finally, he stepped back in front of them. "Thank you," he said. "I hope you continue to make a connection with the spirit of divinity that is within each of us."

After that pleasant experience, Julian advertised a "Quiet Time," which he described as a Sunday connection expressed through meditation, reflection, prayer, and thoughtfulness. It proved popular enough that he could count on four or five people showing up shortly before eleven a.m. on Sundays and sitting respectfully in meeting-house style silence. Some people commented to him that it was the only peace they had throughout the entire week. Some began to express a concern for its value in their lives and implied that they were growing dependent on that quiet time. The four or five people who came through the door on Sunday morning were not always the same. Most were people visiting Hanapepe for the first time. A few were residents of Koloa or Poipu or other neighboring towns. Some, it turned out, had read about The Celestial Connection in a Hawaiian guidebook.

The woman who advertised her estrogen returned one Friday morning before he and Wakea arrived. She was wearing an orange T-shirt emblazoned with "Keep well back! Powered by Estrogen!" She had a worried look. "I was afraid you were not coming," she said.

When he opened the door, she entered and sat on the first bench while he put on the lights and straightened the mess on his desk. Wakea headed for his bowl of water, then curled up near her. Julian had finished his chapbook on the apocalypse and had several bundles of them on the floor. He busied himself with untying the nearest stack and placing a supply of them next to the last, dove-gray, handset.

"I heard you talk about the spirit within."

"Right. It is illuminated by God in everyone."

"Not everyone," she said.

"Do you not feel it in yourself?"

"No, I do feel it. Yes. But it's my mother."

Julian listened to the woman closely. Her mother was somehow out of touch. She was in what the woman described as "the darkness." It took the woman some time, but she eventually convinced Julian to come with her and minister to her mother. This was not something Julian wanted to do. He was much more comfortable in his own space on Hanapepe Road. He would have preferred to stay where he was, but the woman was persuasive. She convinced him that her mother could not come to her, that regardless of his insufficiencies he needed to come to their home and spend at least time enough to say a prayer together. Julian looked at the woman and contemplated for an instant the significance of her T-shirt's motto. He decided this was not estrogen related, and ultimately agreed to come with her.

What he found in the sunny cottage up near Russian Fort surprised him. The woman took him into a darkened bedroom and began crying. Julian saw the mother lying under the cream-colored quilt. Her eyes were closed. Her head was visible and one arm lay outside the quilt. She had steel-gray hair and a slack look to her face.

"She's been this way," the woman said.

"Have you called a doctor?"

"I called you," she said. "People say you have a healing spirit."

It was the first he had heard such a comment. He looked at the mother and wondered what he should do. "What is her name?"

"Just call her 'Mother.'"

He bent over the woman and reluctantly called out, "Mother?" hoping she would respond. But she did not. He touched her arm. The skin felt leathery and cool. He reached for a pulse but got nothing, but then he often failed to get his own pulse. He wasn't sure that proved anything. As he lay his hand on the mother's forehead the woman fell to her knees beside him. In a moment, he, too, fell to his knees and the two of them recited the Lord's Prayer together. Wakea sat between then and observed the mother on the bed. Wakea sniffed loudly and whimpered. He pawed the quilt and held that pose while they kneeled next to him.

"Touch her head again," the woman said.

Julian didn't know what to make of this woman. She was very bossy, and he wondered if it was the estrogen talking.

"Touch her head," she commanded.

Julian lay his hand on the mother's forehead and said the Lord's Prayer again. This time the woman did not join him. She knelt by his side and softly intoned a musical prayer that was in another language, possibly Hawaiian. It had not occurred to him until then that both these women were Hawaiian, or perhaps half Hawaiian. Both had long, graying hair, and both were tanned. He said the Lord's Prayer yet again, then remembered Jesus's words when he raised Lazarus and adapted them for the occasion, "I am the resurrection and the life: she that believeth in me, though she were dead, yet shall she live."

Nothing happened.

He rose and went back into the bright living room and looked out the window at the road below. He had no idea why he had come, what he was doing. He had no idea who this woman was. While he stood there looking out the window, the woman came out of the bedroom and pulled the door to. She seemed calmer, more controlled. "Will you have some iced tea?"

Ordinarily he might have said no, but he nodded.

She placed the tea on the table and he sat across from her. "This place has become almost a spiritual wilderness," she said. "I knew that a long time ago, but I didn't think it would matter."

"We sometimes lose our way," he said.

"I have not lost my way. It is the others who have lost their way. Everything is designed for the worship of money." He wondered for a moment whether she was not quoting one of his chapbooks back to him. "I thought you were just another salesman when I first saw you."

"I'm not a salesman. Not anymore."

"No. I realize that. But once this was one of the sacred places of the island and people were reverent. I bought this house here because the Menehune once blessed this side of the island and I felt close to them.

Julian told her of his forebears, how they came to the island and built the first churches and welcomed the islanders and taught them the word of God. He told how they converted the islanders and brought them into the fellowship of the church and helped them avoid the dangerous practices of their fiery religion. The woman simply nodded. He decided to tell her nothing more of the early church, but rather explained how he had come to Hanapepe and how he had decided to open The Celestial Connection.

The woman in turn talked about her mother and how she had preserved some of the old ways, performing some of the old ceremonies in their home. Yet, she also read the Christian Bible and knew the great prayers by heart. "She dedicated her life to the simplicity of God."

Julian meditated on the word, "simplicity."

"She never worried about sin, or purity, or how others should

175

live. She worried only about perceiving God as directly as any person could."

"How long has she been like this?"

"A month," the woman said. "She hasn't changed in a month."

"You should have called a doctor. I think you need to call a doctor right now."

"We have no doctor."

Julian had met people here who would never see a doctor. He thought he understood their position, but he could hardly sympathize with it. The woman in the other room, he knew full well, was far beyond the help of a doctor. He was thinking these very words, although unable to say them aloud, when from the other room they heard a raspy, old woman's voice call out for her daughter.

The resurrection of Mother Mahuna forced Julian to close The Celestial Connection for more than a week. Curious tourists knocked on his door, stood in front of his brilliant windows, and asked questions up and down the street. Local business was even brisker than usual and the Café Espresso took reservations for lunch and dinner days in advance. Julian and Wakea holed up in their digs and tried to sort out the events. Julian knew he had done nothing to Mother Mahuna. He touched her forehead, yes, but it was cold and unresponsive. He knelt by her side and prayed, but could that have brought her back? He was convinced that she was definitely not dead when he first saw her. She may have been in some strange suspended state, or maybe she was just asleep. It was luck that he was there when she woke up.

A few reporters interviewed Dorothy Mahuna, who showed up on television with yet another T-shirt warning people to keep back, and said that whatever Julian Kusaka and his dog Wakea had done, it saved her mother. Julian got some calls from old advertising friends in Honolulu who expressed surprise at hearing his name on the local news. Many of them congratulated him on doing something worthwhile that they themselves would have enjoyed doing, if only they could afford it.

The newshounds grew weary of the story very quickly, especially in light of an impending strike in Pearl Harbor and the arrival of several dignitaries from Washington visiting the Islands on a political junket. Julian was finally able to return to his chapel and talk with visitors, some of whom knew nothing whatever about Mother Mahuna. Those who did were almost reverent.

"How did you save that woman's life?"

"She was alive already," he protested. "She was just asleep. I didn't save her life." For someone who had attracted attention to products of all kinds, Julian felt the irony of trying to avoid attention. It was not that he would have been unwilling to accept credit for Mother Mahuna's revival, but only that he knew he had no hand in what had happened. Credit where credit is due, was an old motto of his. And he was not due any credit.

Someone decided that Wakea must have been the catalyst for Mother Mahuna's come-back, and whoever it was spread the rumor that Wakea had licked Mother Mahuna's cheeks and brought her back to life. Julian tried to scotch that rumor immediately. When people came into the chapel, they often headed for Wakea and patted his head before moving over to the telephones and listening to Julian's messages. He busied himself in revising the recorded messages, changing them so that repeat visitors would not be disappointed. The phone lines, he told some of them, were filled with news. He tried to keep it news.

Several people asked him to minister to sick friends. He refused all such inquiries. He told them very clearly that they should put their trust in their doctor, not in him or in Wakea. Yet, they persisted. One day an old man with jaundiced eyes and strange skin was wheeled through the doors and placed in front of his desk. Julian was working on a new version of the message he had recorded for the conversion of St. Paul.

"The doctors have given up on him. We need you." The man who spoke those words placed a blank check on the desk in front of Julian. "What are your fees?"

"I have no fees. I don't take fees." He stared at the old man, whose eyes saw little if anything. One of his eyes was cocked toward the ceiling. The other seemed milky and crusted over. Wakea stood at attention and watched the old man.

"Well, take some money for the chapel. You must be able to use it. Just see my uncle for a minute. Say a prayer. Whatever it is you do."

Julian felt as if this young man were speaking to him in the same fashion as he would speak to his plumber. "I don't do anything." He gestured to the bank of telephones. "See if God is calling you," he said. The man looked at him, furious. "I mean it."

The man wheeled his uncle to the phone bank and put a telephone in his hand and helped him hold it to his ear. Wakea moved next to the man and sat beside him. He had picked the phone under the portrait of Jesus and Wakea. After the old man listened to the entire message, his son wheeled him out. Julian hoped he would hear nothing more of him.

A crippled boy was brought in by his parents the following day. Wakea nosed him and the boy rubbed his head. "Use the violet telephone," Julian said. The boy's mother stared at him for an instant, trying to see quite what he meant, then moved the boy to the telephone. She picked it up and listened for a moment. "Put it down," Julian said. "Then pick it up and hold it to your boy's ear. It's for him. See if God is calling him." The woman did as she was told.

Later that week a Japanese couple brought in a little girl whose face was misshapen. The girl squatted down and played with

Wakea before the parents were able to communicate with Julian. He had never learned any Japanese, despite doing business for years in Honolulu, so when the parents began talking, he simply held up his hands in protest. "I don't speak Japanese," he said, knowing they could not understand him. The girl rubbed Wakea's belly, then massaged him under his chin. Wakea held up his forepaws and received the ministration with pleasure. "Go over to the amethyst telephone," he said. He got up and gestured to the telephone beneath the portrait of St. Paul on the sea turtle, and the little girl picked it up. He helped her put it to her ear, making a sign that she should listen. "See if God is calling you," he said, realizing that not only could she not understand him, but that she could not understand what was being said on the telephone.

Julian waited until she put the telephone down. She had listened to the entire message. He gave her the chapbook that lay beside the telephone and held her hand for a moment. She smiled at him and said a few words, to which he nodded. He then placed his hand on her soft black hair and smiled. Her parents bowed and smiled and took her hand. Her mother picked up the dove gray telephone and listened to its message with no apparent comprehension.

The Sunday quiet time attracted a standing-room only crowd. Julian always said a few words, and he did his best to prevent people from talking about Mother Mahuna or any of the other ill persons. He spent time reading in Jeremy Taylor's chapters on "Visitation of the Sick," and frequently ended the eleven o'clock meeting with a simple prayer from chapter five, "O spare us a little, that we may recover our strength before we go hence and be no more seen." That seemed to be a reviving thought for many in the crowd.

When Julian had the chapel to himself, usually for a few minutes early in the morning or late in the day, he tried to spend some time in meditation, often in conference with Wakea. "What good we have done," he told Wakea, "is not ours alone to claim. In fact, I am not sure we have done any good at all." He listened to himself in the empty room and began to worry that he was sounding pompous, preacherly, even when speaking with Wakea. Wakea always listened attentively, looking at Julian's face as if he understood what he was saying, but Julian knew he was probably no more understanding than the poor Japanese girl whose face was painfully distorted. He tried to think about his situation calmly. "I think God is with us, Wakea. Whatever is happening must be for a good reason. But neither of us can take credit for anyone who gets better or even comes back from the dead. If these things are really happening, then we need to be able to step aside and let God work things in His own way. I hope you feel as buoyant in spirit as I do, as you have helped me feel." Wakea stretched out on the floor and drifted off to sleep.

Dorothy Mahuna was a frequent visitor. She had taken to wearing a colorful suite of dresses with floral patterns. This decision somehow calmed Julian. Dorothy apologized for the television coverage. "I didn't know how to say no, if you know what I mean." It surprised her to think that Julian did not want the publicity which she felt he had honestly earned. She tried to understand him. She told him about how her mother was now talking sensibly. The period of her sickness was essentially a blank in her life, although she has a distinct recollection of Julian's dog nuzzling her hand while she was "away," as she called it. When Dorothy came for a visit, she listened to one of the telephones, choosing a different one each time. Today she listened to the saffron phone beneath the painting of Jesus and Wakea. As she listened she smiled at Wakea, who stood near her. Dorothy usually waited for Julian to point to the phone bank and say, "Is God calling you?" But she sometimes pre-empted him and got to the phones before he could say anything.

Stories began to circulate. Locals referred to Julian as a curandero, a term they borrowed from the usage of American Indians, and which they had in turn borrowed from Spaniards in early sixteenth-century Texas. He heard references to his having a "touch" that somehow healed. He also read apocryphal stories of himself as having seen God walking out of the surf at Waikiki, or as having detected the presence of God in his dog, or as having forsaken the world of tangible pleasures because of having received a long-distance telephone call from Jesus in modern Nazareth. Such stories were enticing, but he resisted them all. However, he told Wakea that he understood now how less committed people could begin to believe the fanciful stories others told about them. Creating myths had been his stock in trade for years, but he never truly understood the power of myth until now. If he were not careful, he told Wakea, he might begin believing what people said about him.

The most painful aspect of his great success was his sense that the presence of God was less palpable to him now than when he first established The Celestial Connection. In those early days he felt himself communicating with God on a daily basis. The feeling was akin to a euphoria unlike anything else he had ever known. He felt bathed in a beatific glow, as the angels closest to God were described in the Bible. After years of suppression, he was like a person who understood the world only in terms of feeling. Now, however, with blind women and men finding their way through his doors hoping for the restoration of their sight, the sense that he was one with God had long disappeared. Instead, he felt much as he had when working at Ilima Advertising—distracted by other people's demands.

No one was more demanding than the sick and the blind.

Eventually, Julian hit upon the idea of going on a religious retreat. He had heard how the great early fathers of the church withdrew to a suitable cave or mountainside where they could have God all to themselves. He set out early one morning with enough canned food to last for a week. He knew he could find a place in Waimea Canyon with a supply of water. There were, after all, campsites and trails that the state maintained, although he had never actually seen them. He wanted to make this experience as meaningful and authentic as he could, so he decided that he and Wakea would walk until they found the spot in which they might find the solace they needed.

The result at first was painful. The seven-mile walk from Hanapepe to Waimea Canyon Drive took them three hours, and by the time they began the remarkable ascent of the road, Julian was partially lame. He had never walked seriously before and misjudged the intensity of the experience. Even Wakea was hobbled by the time they began up the canyon road.

A number of cars passed them at considerable speed. One young woman stopped and asked them if they needed a ride. Julian thought about it for a moment, then decided that accepting a ride might defeat the purpose of their retreat. Another hour later, having gone little more than an additional mile, Wakea lay down in the sun and panted vigorously. He needed water, and while Julian had sufficient Alpo, he had no water with him. He realized that if Wakea was as thirsty as he, then they were in trouble. Julian could punish his own body, but it was not fair to punish Wakea.

The young man who picked them up was on his way to the Kokee campsite. He had some bottled water which he shared with Julian and Wakea. Julian was grateful to hear that the campsite had a restaurant and cabins. And while this was not quite his idea of a religious retreat, it was immensely welcome.

No one knew Julian in the State Park. There were a number of young people with their families. One family, in a nearby cabin invited him to join them in their cookout. They had brought coolers with hotdogs and hamburgers. He was impressed at their preparation for camping out, something he had never done before. He decided not to ask his hosts, the Oradells from Milwaukee, whether God was calling them. He was afraid that he might frighten them off, or, worse, that they would have heard of him and then reveal his identity to other campers.

During the day, he and Wakea walked the trails and drank in the intense beauty of the canyon. The sunlight played wonderfully on the distant walls, and they could see the mountain goats scamper across the peaks far away. In the evening, Julian read by a small flashlight he had packed in with the Alpo. He was reading about sin and forgiveness in Jeremy Taylor, and he realized that while God was very real to him, sin was less manifest. He seemed himself as remote from the commission of sin as was Wakea. They made a remarkable pair, he thought.

By the end of the week, Julian's aches and pains were gone. His head was clearer, his communion with God more intense. He realized that he had to learn to balance his own needs with those of the visitors to The Celestial Connection. He had not become close to God to be a servant to others. In reflection, he realized he might appear selfish in his thinking. But his own Godly needs came first. As in everything, he had to find a way to balance his life.

The Oradells gave him a ride down the Canyon Drive and dropped him off at the entrance to Hanapepe Road. They were a happy family, the children filled with stories, entranced by Wakea, and the parents overflowing with their sense of wonder at the landscape. They loved the sky, the canyon, the sea.

Julian decided, as he walked into town, that he must make changes. He was ordinarily in The Celestial Connection during standard business hours, from nine to five, with shortened hours on Sunday. He decided that he would now open in the morning and keep his afternoons free for reflection.

In Waimea Canyon, the sunsets were among the most spiritual of all the phenomena he saw. Each evening, he and Wakea would find a position from which they could view the sunsets through the trees, then turn after the sun had disappeared and watch the light fade on the opposite canyon wall. He began to realize why people could become sun worshipers, how the sun could metaphorize not only life, but God himself. At the end of the week, he felt that God had filled him with strength, that he had been renewed.

It was a shock, then, to find a small collection of notes taped to his door. They were from a variety of people with major ailments. Some, however, were put there by people who claimed to have been cured by him. One woman, who said she was blind when she came and felt Wakea breathing on her, said she was now able to see light and dark and that she detected slight improvements in her sight every day. Another man said he threw away his wheelchair. Julian had no idea what all this meant. He knew that he had done nothing for these people, so it was not difficult for him to throw the messages aside and walk to his desk. He put the messages that were tacked to the door in the waste basket, then put the cards and envelopes in the middle of the desk. He decided that he would not discard them, but wait for the opportune moment to open them, when he felt ready. Right now, he wanted to keep his astonishing personal sense of peace alive.

Wakea, who had rested at his feet, rose suddenly and moved to the door. He stood watching a group of people moving slowly through the street. Julian went to the door and saw a slow-moving hearse heading to the graveyard. Behind it were several people walking, including Dorothy Mahuna. Behind everyone, two men, wearing woven headbands with three or four feathers jutting up from them, walked barefoot playing island flutes. Their music was mournful, slight, and difficult to make out because the breeze wafted the music in the wrong direction. Julian went out on his steps and watched the procession come toward him. Wakea stood on the road below. As the group came close, he saw Dorothy, walking behind the hearse, suddenly break forth and come rushing at him.

"Where were you?" she screamed. "God was calling you. You weren't here. My mother needed you and you weren't here."

She came at him and pounded on his chest. He had come to the bottom step and with the power of her lunge he fell backward.

"My mother's gone," she screamed. She turned to the stunned procession. "Stop the car!" she commanded. "Get them to stop the car."

She pulled at Julian's shirtfront until it began to unseam. "Get up! Get up!"

He got up and pushed his shirt back into his trousers. "What's happened?"

Dorothy grabbed his belt and pulled him roughly into the road and down to the hearse. "Open it!" she cried to the amazed driver. "Open it!"

The driver got out of the hearse and came to the rear, where Dorothy had pulled Julian. "Open the back door!" Finally, the driver realized what she wanted. His assistant, a sallow looking older bald-headed man had gotten out and stood now near the door. He opened it with a sense of ceremony. "Open it up," she demanded, pointing to her mother's casket. "Now!"

"We can't," the older man said.

"I said open it. It's my mother. I paid for the casket. I say open it up."

"It's because," the younger driver said, "we don't have the room when it's inside the hearse."

"Then pull it out! You've got that carriage thing. Pull it out now!"

They both looked at her and then at Julian, whose belt was still in her hand, and began the process of rolling the casket back. As they did so the wheels of the carriage lowered to the road and in a moment the casket was standing there in the middle of the street in the bright morning sun. People began to wander from the restaurant and the galleries. Others stopped their cars and came to see what was happening.

"Dorothy, this is . . .," but she stopped Julian. Wakea stood beside them looking at the brown metal casket.

"Open it."

The two men in their black livery looked at each other. The older man reached into his pocket for a tool and began unscrewing the lid. "We shouldn't be doing this," he said.

"I don't care. Do as I say."

Finally the lid of the casket was up and Mother Mahuna was there, obviously dislodged from her original pose. The older man said something about "settling," and reached in to push her back into a more appropriate position, something suggesting a peaceful repose.

"Now do something!" she ordered Julian. "Bring her back!"

"I can't . . . ."

"Don't tell me you can't. You almost didn't help me the last time. I had to come and get you. This time I came and you weren't here. You could have brought her back."

The crowd began to murmur in her support. Julian heard people say, "Bring her back." "Do something." "Where were you?" "Get the dog in on it." "For God's sake, help her." In the background, he heard the distant sad tunes of the two feathered men playing throughout all the disorder. He finally pulled himself together and dislodged himself from Dorothy. He looked down on Mother Mahuna. She looked astonishingly well. Her face was brighter than he had remembered it from his visit to her darkened bedroom all those months ago. She actually looked more healthy and alive now than she had at that time. As he leaned over the casket, Wakea rose on his hind feet and perched beside him, looking in at Mother Mahuna. The crowd gasped when the dog rose to look, as if they thought the dog was going to make some kind of declaration.

Julian touched Mother Mahuna's forehead. It was cold, hard, unyielding. Some of the funerary makeup was melting in the direct sun and came off on his hand. He saw that her hair was gelled into

186

place and that tiny threads kept her eyelids closed. He heard the crowd behind him urging him to bring her back to life. They were becoming agitated. The flute players came close behind Julian and when they picked up their tune again Wakea, apparently able now to hear them, raised his head and howled like a wolf as they played. The louder they played the louder he wailed. He seemed to be the chief mourner, setting the mood for everyone else.

"Please," Julian cried out, holding up his hand. Wakea moaned. "Please stop playing," he said to the feathered men. "Let me pray. All of you. We will recite the twenty-third psalm." Julian began and, to his surprise, enough of the crowd knew the psalm so that he could lead them through it and then turn his attention to Mother Mahuna, whose make-up was beginning to look a bit more plastic than when the lid was first opened.

He placed his hand on her head again and with his other hand, lifted Dorothy's arm in the air. He turned to the crowd and said, "God is calling Mother Mahuna. I can hear Him on the line. He is calling her to dine with Him now at the great feast in the Celestial City of Light. Can you hear Him? Can you hear Him? I can hear Him calling for Mother Mahuna. Let the Lord be praised. God is on the line."

Wakea lowered himself to the ground and the funeral attendant hastily screwed the coffin lid in place lest the sun damage any more of his work. Dorothy glared at Julian, who still held up her hand as if she were a prize fighter retaining her championship. "Glory to the Lord," Julian said, knowing that tomorrow he would put the place up for sale and search for an even more remote island where no one, if he were cunning, would discover who he really was.

Old Bones

The only thing that surprised him about Francine was her insistence that she had lived past lives in foreign places.

In all other respects, she was charming, sophisticated, and sensible. She wore simple, expensive clothes and built a house on the far side of the highway in a gated community called Everwell Heights. Her husband's death was a shock, despite his having lingered for several years with a blood disorder that gave him great pain and robbed him of his wonderful sense of humor.

When he first met her, Anthony Mirabella found her irresistible. He saw her sitting at the bar in the middle of a July evening out on the noisy deck of the Yacht Club. They were in the middle of a hospital benefit but neither of them wanted to dance, and after watching her order her second margarita, Anthony decided she was alone and that he had a chance if he would only speak up.

"We've not met," he said, moving his Chivas along the bar down to where she sat.

"Yes, but I know you," she said. Her voice had a pleasant rasp. "You sold my neighbor's house. The Kanagawas?"

He nodded. "The Heights."

"I'm number twenty-four."

"With the ship sculpture."

"My husband's." She took a sip of her drink. "He bought it not long before he died. He always wanted something very modern, a bit scandalous. But I don't think it's scandalous. Do you?"

"Interesting is what people usually say. Not scandalous."

"I wanted him to buy one of those realistic pieces, like a

policeman with a drawn revolver."

"That might have been practical, I suppose."

"He thought it was whimsical, but derivative. Martin wanted something representing our boat, The Kapalua Girl, under full sail."

"Except for the fact that it's white, it looks like a Calder."

"It's a Robishaw. From right down in Lahaina. He did a great job."

He would have taken her home that evening except for the logistics of the two cars and the early call he had with people in from San Diego looking at some condos he had been trying to unload for almost a year. But he took her number and promised that he would call her so they could find a nice place for dinner. Francine was pleased that he had admired "The Breezes," as Martin always called their place, especially after Peter Robishaw installed the huge steel structure on their lawn. It always made her think of their carefree days racing into the wind.

Anthony did not sell any of the condos he showed that next day. In some ways he thought the family that had called him was more interested in gushing over Maui than in buying real estate. He emphasized how valuable a condominium could be to someone from San Diego. The rental income could pay for the place if they were to plan carefully. Investing in condominiums, he explained, had made a number of people on the island wealthy.

When he called Francine that afternoon, the machine answered and he decided not to leave a message. People complained to him about not leaving a message, but that was how he was, and that was how he wanted to be.

They eventually caught up with each other on Friday. Anthony left the agency early and went to Floral Expectations for an arrangement with Bird of Paradise at the center, something dramatic. There were flowers all around him, but he knew the names of very few. But the florists knew the names, and his flowers always came from a downtown refrigerated display.

"Lovely," Francine said. She placed them near the kitchen sink and reached for a large crystal vase. She arranged the flowers and placed them on a fluted stand in the living room. "Can you make us a drink? We'll go out on the deck and watch the sunset. Are you a sun-worshiper?"

"Of course." He iced the shaker and found the Bombay gin and vermouth. She placed some brie and water biscuits on a tray and led him through the living room to the deck, which was filled with orchids, some hanging from above, some on their own stands, some on a low table. The effect was interesting, almost exotic.

"You have a lovely place," he said.

"What I like most is the view at sunset. Martin and I always stopped everything and sat out here to watch the sun go down. It was often spectacular. The way it is going to be tonight."

Anthony positioned his chair and sat next to her. "I sometimes see the sun rise. Do you often see the sun rise?"

"Not really."

"The beginnings of things impress me, I suppose. When a day comes to an end I like to feel that something has been accomplished."

"When the day ends the evening begins," she said. She raised her glass in a salute.

They sat and watched the sun tint the clouds low on the horizon. The color spread across the sky, deepening, shifting, radiating in a brilliant display. Anthony enjoyed the opportunity to relax, to put up his legs and forget everything but the moment.

"When I see the sun like this," she said, "I think of the long, intense Egyptian evenings in Luxor."

"You've been to Egypt?"

"Not in this life, but long ago."

He studied her features. She did not look Egyptian. "Long ago," he said.

190

"Yes. You know how some people say they were pharaohs or princesses in ancient Egypt. I thought that was strange. But I've discovered I was a priestess of the cult of the goddess Isis. Her son was Horus. I named my own son Horace. I never knew why."

"Isis?"

"Yes, she was very powerful. The god Ra was the most powerful, of course. That was the sun god."

"Ah. And you sense that you were once a priestess."

"I know it. Yes. Does it sound odd to you?"

"I suppose a little."

"Since I was a child I had the awareness. That's what made me listen so closely to Kara Monson. You know, she gives consultations downtown. We'll have to go one of these days. You may be surprised what you will learn about yourself."

He repressed a snort. "I'm always surprised to learn about myself."

Because of their talk about Francine's awareness, they decided to go to Kimo's that evening. As they walked past Kara Monson's discreet sign, "By Appointment," Anthony looked above to see softly lighted windows. Consultations tonight, he thought. It was difficult for him to accept the idea of a past life, but Francine was obviously convinced that she had at least one, and possibly more. It wasn't the kind of conversation he had hoped to have with her, but he found it impossible to stray very far from what was on her mind.

"It's very important," she said over their risotto, "that you share my knowledge about past lives."

He filled his mouth with a timely bite and nodded.

"Because it is the kind of thing that could come between friends if they are not sympathetic."

"I try to keep an open mind."

"Of course. I can tell that already."

"So, you feel that you had more than one past life?"

She smiled. "That is what is so extraordinary. There have been more than I can count. I'm very clear on my Egyptian sojourn. I was untrue to my vows of the cult and buried in a grove of date trees sacred to Isis."

"Buried?"

"Alive. You can't imagine how I felt when I realized the source of my claustrophobia. It was the most liberating experience, although I still find it difficult to walk into elevators unless the light is bright. Now we are working on my life in Bethany."

"Which is?"

"Bethany is near Bethlehem and Jerusalem. Kara and I have been working on this for some time. We've worked out that I ran a food business of some kind in Bethany. I had a husband, that much is clear. And I had a gift. We can see that, too. It was a gift for making food delicious, apparently a knowledge of seasoning."

"Seasoning would do it," he said, hoping he did not sound dismissive.

"Kara thinks we may have catered the last supper. If that was true, then I would have known Jesus. But not intimately, of course."

"And you would have been Jewish."

"Isn't it an exciting thought?"

Anthony ruminated on the idea throughout the evening. One of his great fears was becoming involved with a crazy woman. "Meshugah," his friend Morris Besor said when he thought someone a bit squirrely. Craziness was difficult because Anthony had no way of coping with anyone who heard voices, shouted shrilly, or cried hysterically.

It was partly to avoid such women that Anthony had worked his way west. His wife was diagnosed as manic-depressive, and after the still-birth of their child she cycled wildly between the highs and the lows, driving him almost crazy. The divorce saved them both, especially after she began taking her lithium. The settlement specified that alimony would end when she remarried, which she did after three years. He never wanted to chance that kind of anxiety again.

When the evening ended–with a discreet kiss on the driveway–he went back to his apartment and poured himself a scotch and tried to think things through. Flipping through his Modern Library Freud, he saw nothing on past lives. But Freud's comments on *déjà vu* reassured him. The sense of a past life was much the same, and Freud admitted to feelings of *déjà vu* himself. He attributed them to childhood experience and treated them as normal.

Anthony closed the book with a sense of relief. There was nothing normal about thinking you lived in ancient Luxor or Biblical Bethany, but if Freud's analysis held water, then it was possible that the experience was related to some trauma in this life, such as a repressed fear of being buried alive linked to a childhood experience. It could be that Francine had seen a coffin lowered into the ground as a child. Perhaps her repressed fear was sublimated and recycled as a belief that she was a naughty priestess caught *in flagrante* who paid the ultimate price for love.

Throughout the week, Anthony concentrated on developing his own awareness, trying to recover some evidence of a past life.

He had several clients looking for condos with nice views of the water, and since his had nice views of a pleasant neighborhood, or nice views of an indifferent hole on a golf course, he tried his best to emphasize the values involved in staying back from the water. He showed the condos even though he knew it was an uphill battle, and in one case he thought there might be a deal in the making. The husband of one couple began talking about how they should take up golf now that they were in an environment in which they could play almost every day. He reminded his wife that they had played when they were younger, that they could probably find their clubs, and that it would be good for them to get out and stroll the links. Anthony did not mention that the "links" required their using carts to speed up play.

The week's effort produced no specific awareness in him. He thought that if he had ever had a past life that it might have involved being a stonemason or selling real estate. His father once said that no one ever grows up hoping to become a real estate salesman. Anthony responded by saying he had never heard a child tell a parent that he wanted to become a stonemason, either. But for his father masonry was real work with a real product, while real estate involved nothing much more than talk. Anthony said, however, that the product of real estate sales was money, often a great deal of it.

One evening he sat down with a drink after dinner and leafed through a picture book on Italy thinking that if he had a past life, maybe it would have been in Florence or Mantua during the great flowering of learning. He tried to imagine himself as an architect, someone like Brunelleschi building the great *duomo*. Could he have helped build it? Perhaps he had been a mason. Masonry was the family business in Italy back to the nineteenth century, and probably centuries before that.

It was logical that if he had had an earlier life, it would have been in Italy. Perhaps he had lived in Rome in the time of Augustus Caesar. He turned to views of the Roman Forum, searching for clues, something to jog the memory. This, at least, he reasoned, was a possibility. Maybe he had been a stone mason building the great aqueducts that supported Rome. Or perhaps he had helped build the Colosseum. When he thought about it, it occurred to him that he could have sold a country estate to Seneca or one of his friends. They must have had land agents in those days, speculators in real estate.

The possibilities, once he threw himself into the game, were immense, unlimited. He could have been a senator in Rome, a centurion in Verona, a tavern keeper in Capri, a merchant in Amalfi. But the more he thought about it, the more he was convinced that if there were such things as past lives, that they would have been embedded in his genes. He gave no credence to having been an insect or animal–or that he was destined to be one. No, he would have been an ancient Italian of some kind. He might even have been a distant relative and have shared some of his present genes with a hundred antecedents. That idea satisfied him partly because it was elegantly simple, and partly because it permitted him to think in terms of continuity on the genetic level.

By the time he went to bed, he felt much more confident that Francine's beliefs were not ludicrous or off the wall. There could be something to them, and he felt better about her most recent suggestion that they share an audience with Kara Monson.

By the time Madame Monson was able to book them in, Anthony considered the issue of past lives with more equanimity than when he first heard Francine talk about Luxor and the cult of Isis. He had even grown curious. None of the women in his office had heard of Kara Monson. None of the men had the faintest idea who she was or what she did. Once or twice he dropped a hint about past lives with potential clients hoping that possibly one of them would pick up the idea and shed a bit of light on it for him. But apparently none of them had given the idea much–or any–thought.

Francine looked dazzling when he picked her up. They went downtown to the Fish House for dinner. He ordered a white burgundy, very full bodied, with their seafood. They had had their cocktails earlier watching the sunset, but Anthony ordered a scotch before dinner while searching through the new menu. He felt very good when they had their coffee.

They walked into the cool dark street and saw the street alive with activity. It was Friday, and Kara Monson wanted to see them around ten-thirty.

Anthony was not sure, in retrospect, what he expected. Maybe a crystal ball, or an emblem of enchantment on the wall, or a black cat slithering behind the curtains at opportune moments. But none of that. Instead, Kara Monson showed them into a small studio room with a desk, a wall of books, many of which looked interesting, and several soft leather chairs. Behind the desk was a fireplace that had seen recent use. It contained a small pile of wood and paper.

Anthony waited politely while Francine and Kara bussed one another and held out his hand when Francine introduced him. Kara Monson was a dark-haired woman of unusual height wearing a dark silk dress and dark shoes. She had on no makeup and no visible jewelry except for a handsome silver pin on her lapel. If he had not been prepared, he might have assumed he was visiting a psychotherapist.

He actually said as much and was stunned when he heard Kara Monson tell him, "Oh, yes. I was for a long while a practicing therapist. I'm surprised Francine didn't tell you."

"Silly of me," Francine said. "I dropped a stitch."

"You have a Ph.D.?"

"Do degrees give you a sense of security?" She was smiling as she spoke, as if amused at whatever he might say.

"Always," he said with a flourish.

"He's being funny," Francine said.

"We have been doing some interesting work," Kara Monson said. "Has Francine told you about it?"

"The past lives, yes. There's always the possibility of a spiritual conservation of energy thing, isn't there? Just so much spirit to go around throughout the ages. I was thinking about it all week. Looking for signs in my own case."

"But you found none?"

"No. But I was trying to work on my awareness."

"Francine has a deep sense of awareness. Not all people do."

"But you think all people have had past lives."

"I was skeptical, myself," Francine said.

"As you should be." Kara moved behind the desk. Francine

took the chair to their right and he sat in the chair to the left. "It took quite a while for us to begin the process of recovery. As I recall it happened almost by accident, do you remember?"

"Yes, I was incredibly upset. I had bought a new car and found I couldn't sit in it for more than a few moments at a time. I had to drive it with the top down, rain or shine. And then when we talked. . . ."

"Yes," Kara said, sliding a hand in Francine's direction.

Anthony saw how she comforted Francine.

"I wanted you to help Anthony develop an awareness of his own."

"And you'd like that?" she asked him.

"Well, sure. I told you I've been thinking about the past. It stands to reason that I would have had a past life in Italy somewhere, maybe ancient Rome."

"Because of your Italian background."

"Because everyone in my family is Italian. Doesn't that make sense to you?"

"Tell me a little about yourself."

Anthony hesitated, wondering just what might be of interest to her, then began telling her about his family, how his father was very tough and distant when he was younger, how his older brother looked after him, how his mother seemed at times to resent him. It was a drab tale.

"What are you most afraid of?"

He thought for a moment. "I'm not sure. Dying young? Being dependent on others? I don't know."

"Do you swim?"

"No." He was surprised at the question.

"Ah. How do you feel about drowning?"

"I'm against it," he said with a laugh.

"Seriously."

"I guess you're right. That's something I really fear."

"Have you had a bad experience in the water?"

"Yes. How could you tell?"

"And you almost drowned when you were a child. Did your brother save you?"

"My God, he did. How could you know that?"

"I couldn't. It was implied in what you told me about yourself. It also implies other things about your past. Your deep past."

Anthony was astonished. He had not talked about his experiences as a three-year-old child with anyone. He'd never said a word to Francine about any personal memories. His near drowning was something he had put out of his mind until Kara Monson had dredged it up again.

"I'm going to do something that may be a little strange to you," Kara Monson said. "It is an ancient ritual that predates Christ, and possibly even the Pharaohs. But it is effective." She rose from the desk and turned to the fireplace. She placed a rack over the starter sticks and lighted the fire. It blazed for a moment, then settled down in a steady glow.

Francine squeezed his hand. "This is fascinating," she said.

Anthony watched, wondering why one needed a fire in July. Kara Monson said nothing as they watched the fire catch and sustain itself. When it was ready, she opened a bottom desk drawer and pulled out a rectangular metal container. It was very plain, dark, and apparently old. When she opened it she selected three flat white objects and lay them on the desktop and replaced the box.

"Would you hold these in your hands," she said.

He took them from her. They were cool and smooth, like pieces of ivory. "Are these bones?"

"Yes."

He studied them. They were about three inches long,

198

carefully sawn, rubbed down with pumice or something similar to make them very smooth to the touch. They were flat, possibly rib bones. "Are these human bones?"

"I want you to rub them. First take your forefinger and rub both sides of your nose, then rub the bones with your forefinger. Then I want you to hold them and rub each with your thumbs. Then please put them here." She held out a metal salver. He put them on the plate, then looked quizzically at Francine. She seemed unperturbed.

Kara Monson studied the bones carefully under the light on her desk. He had no idea what she was looking for, but he studied them as carefully as he could from his vantage. She then took the salver and placed it on the rack, then turned to Anthony to explain her procedure.

"The heat will inscribe the bones. You will see dark lines begin to show up in a few minutes. Then you will hear some cracking noise. When that ends, I will remove the bones from the fire and we will study them."

Anthony became aware of the darkness of the office behind him and Francine. They had focused totally on the lamp on Kara Monson's desk and now the light from the fire. The bones grew darker. They sat in silence until they heard the first cracking sound from one of the bones. The process was completely mysterious to him, and he watched Francine for a clue as to how he should respond. She sat rapt and intent.

The second crack came, apparently from a different bone.

The bones were now darker and darker. When the third crack, louder than the first two, sounded, Kara Monson drew in a sigh and removed the salver with tongs. She had placed a thick mat on her desktop and placed the salver on it. She moved the lamp closer to the bones and studied them, one at a time. She did not touch them, nor did she seem very impressed by what she saw.

"What are you looking for?" he asked.

"I could ask you the same question," she said. "But what I see is interesting."

Anthony leaned over and looked at the bones. They were almost caramel-colored and now filled with crackled lines and a few large splits. Francine also leaned over and looked closely. He wondered if she knew any more about what she saw than he.

"These lines," Kara said, pointing with a letter-opener to a set of lines, "are almost like hieroglyphics. They tell a story. What I see here is very suggestive. You see these marks here," she said pointing again. "They suggest the keel of a ship. And these lines suggest a sail. Now, to have these make sense I need to see a similar sign on the other bones. And look here. Here. This replicates the sail on the first bone. And the third bone's most distinct image is right here. A large keel, like an ancient ship. It is the most distinctive image."

Anthony saw the image. It could be a keel, although it was a bit outsized, somewhat square and not very sleek, not what he would think of as seaworthy. He looked for the emblems of sails and with some effort interpreted certain dark cracks as maritime sails. There were many other cracks on all the bones, but they did not seem to form objects in the same ways these marks implied ships and sails.

"What do you think these other marks mean?"

"Perhaps when we have explored the obvious ones, those will become evident."

"It takes time," Francine explained. "With mine, the marks we thought were undecipherable turned out to be foodstuffs and utensils. Once we had the major theme, we learned how to interpret the minor details."

"In some past life," Kara Monson said, "it is very clear that you were a great naval officer, or perhaps a great merchant."

"Or a builder of ships?"

"No, the marks are clear. You see the distances here in these images. That implies sailing great distances over great periods of time. You were a sailor in one of your earlier lives."

"Anthony used to sell yachts in Honolulu," Francine said.

"It just doesn't seem likely to me," he said.

"I think it's pretty plain in the glyphs. You see this," Kara said, pointing to several small signs on the bones. "This is Greek. See the delta and the alpha next to it. What that suggests is a bill of lading for an ancient Greek vessel. You were thinking Italy, but Italy is late in history. The Greeks were great seafarers, and these signs imply some kind of trade. My thought is that you were an ancient Onassis, perhaps. Or perhaps supplying ships to a royal armory."

"All my people were stonemasons. I thought if I were anything it would have been a builder, like my father and his father."

"This is much earlier, before your family came to settle in Italy, before Rome was imagined. This is the time when the Greeks commanded the Mediterranean and established their colonies in present day Turkey and Sicily, not to mention North Africa, where there are still remains of Greek settlements."

He leaned closer to the bones. The marks she pointed to did look like Greek. She pointed to a figure that resembled theta and another that looked like a gamma. It was surprising to see these random signs suddenly take on the forms of the Greek alphabet once Kara began the process.

"If we take these markings and combine them we get a name. I think your name was Deiphobus. Does that ring a bell at all?"

He shook his head. The thought of himself as a Greek was something he was totally unprepared for. Could there be anything to this strange process? "Are you sure of the name?"

"No, not completely. But the markings are clear and there is one very strange thing I see here." He followed her glance. "This mark is a dilemma."

"A problem?"

"No, no. A mark that suggests a sharing. It suggests that

when you were Deiphobus you had a double."

"A twin," Francine said.

"Yes. Do twins run in your family?"

"My father was a twin. But that's all I know about. My mother had a sister, but not a twin."

"It's possible it was not a twin, but a brother, someone very like yourself at that time."

"I don't know," he said. "You can tell all that from these marks?"

"I told you, this is a very ancient practice. I find it very reliable in unlocking secrets. The ancients used it to foretell the future, but I find it more congenial to study the past through the lens of these bones. The past has so much to tell us about ourselves, our present life. And I think our present life is most precious, don't you?"

Francine nodded. "This thing about twins is interesting," Anthony said. "But I can't imagine myself as a Greek."

"This was long ago. Your people must have migrated to Italy before the founding of Rome."

"That's a long time ago." Anthony stared at the bones and decided to ask no more questions. He looked at his watch and Kara Monson saw that he was anxious to leave.

"Perhaps another time," she said. "It is growing late. You've had a great deal to absorb. Francine?"

Francine rose and thanked her. "You've been wonderful."

Anthony sat staring ahead of him. He thought he saw Francine give Kara a check, but she did it so suavely that he may have been wrong. There was no question but that they were very close to one another. He could see that Kara had a profound calming effect on Francine, just as he might expect from a therapist. Yet the entire experience was so far beyond anything that he could have imagined that he was uncertain how he should take it. If someone had told him he would spend the evening looking at bones that had been roasted over a fireplace on Front Street he would have told them they were crazy. Francine, on the other hand, took the entire experience to be quite normal.

Francine drove them back to her house and that evening they made love for the first time. He had the feeling that he had passed an initiation rite and that she now felt she could be truly intimate with him. But at the same time he puzzled through what he had heard from Kara. She had discovered a secret that he would not have gladly divulged. He had been virtually an infant when the accident happened. He had been taken out of the water and given up for dead, but in the hospital he had begun breathing while lying on a gurney in a hallway. His memory of the event was expunged until years later. His father told him very little about the experience, and his brother Aldo had said nothing about it. Aldo had saved him at the risk of his own life. But when he asked Aldo about that day he rarely said more than that it was amazing that Anthony lived, considering how long he had been in the water.

The next morning he called his father to talk about some of the things Kara said. He did not tell him that he had been in a seance, and he certainly said nothing about the bones. Instead, he asked him about the day that he almost drowned. His father did not want to talk about it at first, but eventually he opened up and explained that they had been at a lake in northern Minnesota near where they had lived. But the next thing he told Anthony gave him chills. Aldo had leaped in to haul him out of the dark water, but when he did so he had to make a choice. He chose to let Anthony's sister drown in order to save Anthony.

"What? What sister? You never told me I had a sister."

His father was silent. "Cora Maria," he said softly. "We never talked about her again. It was too painful for your mother. That's why Aldo does not talk about that day. It was a terrible thing to choose one and not the other. And then, we all thought you were dead too. Cora Maria was in the water much longer than you, and she was blue when we got her out. No one knew you two had gone. You were playing, chasing each other and you fell into deep water. It was Aldo who heard you scream. You can't imagine what we went through."

"I had a sister. Was she a twin?"

"She was born eight minutes before you."

"Why did you never tell me?"

"What would be the good? You didn't remember the day you almost drowned until I told you about it many years after. It was as if you had lost your sense of everything that happened in your childhood up to that time. You forgot Cora Maria."

Anthony sat staring at the phone. This was almost more than he could handle. He may not be dredging up a past life in the sense that Francine thought about it, but he definitely dredged up a past that he had repressed in the classic Freudian fashion, through trauma. He had absolutely no memory of a sister, no memory of the day that he fell into the deep water and lost consciousness. Yet, in all the succeeding years he knew enough to take special precautions near the water. When he sold boats, he was the only one to wear a life jacket while demonstrating with a client. Usually the clients were amused, although he feared they might be suspicious of the quality of the boat, because no other broker did that. He did it because a deep instinct pushed him to it. Now it was plain to him why he was so fearful.

When he put the phone down he called his brother Aldo in Eugene. Aldo was an internist at the University hospital. Anthony asked him outright, without even the preliminaries of a hello. Aldo was silent for a long moment.

"What's this about?" he asked.

"When you saved me at the lake. Did I have a sister? Cora Maria?" Anthony heard a strange sound on Aldo's end. "Aldo?"

"My God," Aldo said. His voice was almost indistinct. Then

it was plain that he was weeping.

"Aldo?"

A silence. Then Aldo's voice came on again, weaker, plaintive. "I had to choose. I couldn't see her as plainly as I saw you. I had to choose. Mom never forgave me. Cora Maria was everything to her. You didn't know. I've carried that all these years."

"Jesus, Aldo. That's why nobody ever mentioned it? Nobody ever told me. That's why Mom was so strange with me. What a crazy thing to live with."

"When Mom was dying I asked her to forgive me, but she couldn't. I shouldn't have asked her. They shouldn't have put this on me."

"They gave me up for dead at the hospital."

"Did Dad tell you this?"

"Today, just a few minutes ago. I never knew a thing."

"I'm not sure you were even four years old then. They never had another kid. It was just you and me."

"Why didn't you tell me? I wouldn't even have known about the accident if Dad hadn't told me when I was about fifteen. He never said a word about Cora Maria. I should have been told."

"But you saw her gravestone."

"I thought she was a cousin. She was in Uncle Vito's plot."

"Why is it so important now?"

"It's always been important. Why wasn't I told until now?"

That night Anthony was afraid to go to sleep. He feared he might dream about Cora Maria, his missing half. He feared she might come to him in a dream and demand her life back from him. She deserved a life, the very life that he led. Aldo's decision to save him instead of her was arbitrary–or at least it seemed to have been arbitrary to Aldo. He went after Anthony because he was more clearly visible, while Cora Maria had already sunk beneath the earthy waters. And all these years he lived with the sense that his mother resented much of what he did and who he was. She always held back her emotions from him. He never worried about it, except to feel that his mother had a limitation that, from what he could tell from seeing other parents, was fairly normal. Now it was a little clearer to him.

He did not dream about Cora Maria. Instead, he dreamt of sailing empty seas. In his dream he heard the opening words from Verdi's *Otello*: *"Una vela,"* repeated over and over. However, he was not looking at the sail, he was behind the sail, homing in, but never getting closer. He was on a ship that would never get to port.

That morning he went out on his small deck with a cup of instant coffee and sat watching the sun rise, breaking through the cobalt clouds like a torch. Birds sang nearby and far away he heard the early morning traffic going up the coast. He felt his life was not really his own any more. And he felt his life was much less than it might have been. He reflected on his failed marriage, the loss of his child, his failure as a boat salesman. What kind of life was it to be a failure on so many levels? He had not sold a condo in two months. But what if he had sold twenty? Would that have been a successful life?

If Cora Maria were to come back somehow and demand of him what was rightfully hers, what might he do? What talents would Cora Maria have had that he did not have? What richer veins of life might she have been able to tap that he could not? Would she not have achieved a life of greater significance, of richer proportions? He thought all these things watching the sun now balancing on the early morning clouds. His life was, to put it plainly, as insignificant, as meaningless as the life of the birds he heard in the trees. Even if he had had a hundred earlier lives, all of them would have been as empty as this. But if Cora Maria had lived, perhaps she might have brought to life a seriousness and a purpose that had eluded him all these years. Why was he saved and she lost? What was it that his mother had grieved for all her life?

The most serious question he had to ask himself frightened him. How could he make his life meaningful? How could he redeem the choice that Aldo made and that his parents never had the courage to face or to tell him about?

Anthony began the day by quitting his job.

He walked into the office and talked with Laura Irigara and explained that he no longer saw his future in real estate. She was shocked, but she did not try to change his mind.

He asked Francine to lunch at the Sunrise Café. She came in wearing a tennis outfit. She was due at the club at one-thirty. It took him only a few minutes to explain to her that he was leaving Hawaii. She was jolted. "I need a drink," she said, signaling the waiter. She got a glass of Merlot and asked him why he was making such a rash decision. "Was it what Kara Monson told you?"

He explained his conversations with his father and with Aldo. He tried to tell her about his feelings and fears concerning his lost sister. "My God," she said, "I never thought . . . ."

"I'm going to have a word with Kara Monson before I go. But I wanted you to know it is not you. It's something about me. Something I see now that I need to do that I should have done a long time ago. If I had known about myself what I know now."

He stayed behind when Francine went off to play tennis. He had another cup of coffee and looked out at people walking down to the water. After a while he walked out and down toward Kimo's and looked for Kara Monson's sign. It was almost two o'clock. He went up the stairs and knocked on the door. He heard nothing for a few moments, then Kara looked out and smiled at him. "Can you wait a minute?" she asked. She signaled toward a captain's chair on the landing. Anthony sat down and studied the waiting area. The rug on the floor was coarse, worn. The floorboards were old and the lower part of the walls was old-fashioned wainscoting. A small square window at the end of the hallway admitted light, but it had not been cleaned for some time. He crossed his legs and waited.

A small blonde woman hastened out of the door and down the stairs without looking at him. The door closed behind her and he thought to rise and knock again, but he decided to wait. It took more than a few minutes for Kara Monson to reappear. She smiled again and held the door open for him. "Did something I said worry you?" she asked.

He walked into the office and sniffed for the smell of roasting bones, but the air was clear. "No. Not directly. Can I level with you?"

She nodded.

"I tried to be open minded, but I have to let you know that I think all this stuff about past lives is bullshit. And I think you know it as well as I do. You're a smart woman and I think you've found a way to make a good living helping people like Francine take their lives a lot more seriously because they think something they did in a past life was really important. They know that nothing they're doing in this life is important at all, so you help them get off the hook by connecting them with great doings in a safe distant environment. And the thing is that I think you could have done that for me, too, if I had been able to persuade myself to be a believer. But I couldn't."

"Is that all you want to tell me?"

"No. First, I want to tell you I think you help people even if you are a fraud. I'm not accusing you of anything and I am not interested in telling anybody else what I am telling you. So you don't need to get worried."

"Do I look worried."

"I told you I think you're very smart. Smart enough not to worry. And so far as I can see you have a remarkable talent that does people some good. I liked Francine and I thought I could make our relationship better by believing the way she believes, but that's not going to happen."

"Maybe you should go."

"What I wanted to tell you is that you opened a door for me. I want to compliment you even though I don't think you're on the level. What you said about a double. You called it a dilemma."

"Yes, it's like a bracket. It's meant to join things."

"Well, I found out I had a kind of double, a twin sister that I never knew. I almost drowned when I was three and I was in the water with my sister. Our older brother dove in and found me first and saved me. He found my sister second, but it was too late by then. Do you know what this means? Can you imagine what it feels like to learn something like this about yourself at my age?"

"It must be a shock. Sit down."

"No. I need to go in a moment. I don't really need you any more. Not to help me. I'm sure you would be good at that, but I really don't need it now. What I learned is that everyone in my family knew this but me. They held it back because they could not face the loss of my sister. She was the jewel of the family, and she died while I lived. Don't you see what I'm saying? The water took her from us. I owe her a life."

"You don't owe her a life."

"You don't understand what I'm saying. I do owe her a life. I owe her a meaningful life, and I have not been living it. I've been hibernating, living a life on hold, here in the sun. I need to go back and see if I can start again and make my life count for something."

"So you think I am a fraud, and yet you've made such a discovery."

"You are a fraud, but you changed my life. I want you to think about that when you roast the next set of bones in your fireplace. What you do and what you say you see really matters to people, so don't take it lightly."

Anthony left Kara Monson without closing the door, imagining her watching him go down the stairs and out into the street.

He had tickets on an Aloha flight to San Francisco, and then he would get a connecting flight to Eugene, Oregon, and he would take some time to talk seriously with his brother and father, and if the rain was not too heavy, he would take a long walk around the university and ask himself how he could shape his talents and energies in directions that would make him worthy of Cora Maria's lost life.

About the Author: Lee Jacobus was Professor of English Literature at the University of Connecticut, Storrs, from 1968 to 2001. His books include *Shakespeare and the Dialectic of Certainty, Sudden Apprehension: Aspects of Knowledge in Paradise Lost, A World of Ideas, The Bedford Introduction to Drama,* and *The Humanities Through the Arts.* His plays include *Fair Warning, Long Division,* and *Dance Therapy.* He is a member of the Dramatists Guild.

His experiences in Hawaii, among almost all the islands, have been intense in their revelation of the inner life of those who live in "paradise."